TRAVIS MORTON AND THE STONES OF ZAR

WARRICK ALLAN FIVAZ

**British Library Cataloguing in Publication
Data**

A Record of this Publication is available from the
British Library.

ISBN: 9798503223408

DEDICATION

This Book Is Dedicated to My Wonderful
and Adoring Children

… Sheldon, Jaden & Shanette …

"KEEP THE IMAGINNATION ALIVE"

TRAVIS MORTON AND THE STONES OF ZAR

CONTENTS

Acknowledgments   i

1   The New House   9

2   Pathfinder   43

3   Trip Through Time   63

4   Way of Trogg   90

5   The Gates of Netherless   111

6   Good Versus Evil   128

7   The Cave of Time   153

8   The Impossible Battle   163

ACKNOWLEDGMENTS

My heartfelt thanks go out to my favorite primary school teacher
Mrs. Richards from
Robert Carruthers Primary in Witbank South Africa
(The best story teller ever)

...

And a wonderful English teacher

PS How is the little red Ferrari?
(Red Mini)

In particular I would like to thank Kevin Beckin for his amazing
artwork

1 CHAPTER NAME

THE NEW HOUSE

Ten-year-old Travis Morton and his family had just moved to Amatikulu, a small village down along the North Coast of Natal, in the heart of Zululand in South Africa. Travis's dad had accepted a job offer to run the local sugar mill there, and things had moved rather quickly after that.

They had only been in Amatikulu for a couple of hours before they were hit with the hottest day the village had seen for well over 20 years; the sun was blistering as it beamed down on the hard, cracked land. Wanting to make the most of the sun, Travis decided to fetch his catapult – plus a couple of marbles – and venture out to explore the gardens of his new home, Eagoli Manner.

Travis Morton was an ace with a catapult, he had been taught how to use a catapult by the gardener and best friend Thulani. Thulani was only 12 years old when they first became friends, which made him five years older than Travis. Thulani spent most weekends looking after the Morton's garden in their previous house. Growing the most amazing vegetables and making the best catapults one could only imagine, Thulani was a master when it came to hunting in the bush with a catapult.

These new gardens of Egoli manner were truly enormous, and the entire estate was surrounded by a large green hedge that seemed to stretch right up into the sky (though in reality was only perhaps 12 foot high) It was covered in tiny red and green peppercorn styled balls.

There were four trees in the garden, though one stood out from the rest; the giant African mulberry tree was situated at the back of the house, at the very bottom end of the garden, and it caught Travis' eye immediately. There was also a little stream that flowed through the estate, and if you looked closely, you could see hundreds of little tadpoles franticly wriggling their bodies to swim around in the crystal-clear waters.

-Egoli Manner-

Travis decided to head straight towards the huge mulberry tree at the bottom of the garden. "Wow – this tree is huge!" Travis muttered to himself. "I can't even see where the top ends, if it even ends at all!"

Looking up through the branches of the tree in awe, Travis spotted a strange-looking bird perched above him. "I bet I can hit that bird with a marble," he mumbled, before loading his catapult, taking aim, and firing. He watched in satisfaction as the bird fluttered and fell to the ground with a thud.

At the age of ten, Travis was a master with the catapult. In fact, he'd been making catapults and using them since he was just six years old, and over the years he'd learned exactly where to hit a bird, and how hard he had to hit in order to stun it.

This time, however, Travis got a little more than he'd bargained for.

"What – what is this?" he stammered. "This isn't a bird! But I could have sworn it was a..." Just then, right in front of Travis' eyes, the creature turned transparent and disappeared. "... A bird," Travis finished in a trembling voice. Kneeling down, he swept his hand over the area at least three times where the thing had fallen, but he couldn't see or feel anything.

By now Travis was starting to get more than a little scared – he felt uneasy and uncomfortable as all kinds of strange thoughts started rushing through his mind.

Just then, he heard a noise by the hedge, and as quickly as he could, he loaded up his catapult and fired it at the foliage.

"Ow, who did that?" a voice yelled out from the opposite side of the hedge.

"Who's that?" asked Travis, intrigued.

"My name is Zarf," came the reply, "and who are you?"

"My name is Travis," he responded, a little hesitantly, before adding, "I can hear you but I can't see you…"

"I don't let anyone see me, especially those who use me as

target practice!" Zarf answered in a stern voice.

"What are you? Where do you come from?" Travis asked, ignoring the harsh tone of Zarf's words – he just wanted answers.

"So many questions for a little soldier!" Zarf replied immediately. "Tell me, who sent you? And where are they now? Let me at them so I can cast a spell on them, turn them into mushrooms and gobble them up!"

Travis couldn't quite believe what he was hearing. "You can do magic and cast spells? Let me see you! Please? I can't answer your questions when I can't even see who it is I'm talking to," Travis stated, rather reasonably.

"I am Zarf the Glebbilin; as a matter of fact, I am the only Glebbilin alive – that I know of – around here." Zarf said the words almost proudly.

Just then Zarf walked out from the hedge, staring at Travis through his beady little eyes. Zarf started to become visible once more showing his true form as the thin, short white bearded little man that he was. Shaking his head, he said, "You have some nerve waking me from my sleep! I was just about to catch a few rays of sunshine when everything went dark. I ended up in the hedge after being shot with that thing in your hands... WHAT IS THAT?"

"It's a catapult," replied Travis, "and I'm sorry for shooting you with it, but I thought you were a bird," he explained.

"You thought I was a bird?" Zarf asked incredulously. "And what gives you the right to go around shooting birds out of trees?"

"Nothing I guess," shrugged Travis. "Anyway, what are you doing in my tree and where did you come from?" He was eager to get back to asking some questions himself.

"I come from Netherless land of Glebbilins, and have been here for the last two days," Zarf replied, as if what he was saying was completely normal. "I need to find the Great Stones and return with them to my kind. Back to my own time."

"Your own time – you mean you're from *another* time? Another world?" Travis asked, his mouth hanging open.

"Yes, I was sent by Hop the great Wott of Netherless land to retrieve the Great Stones of Zar, which were stolen by Murtic, the evillest half-Glebbilin half-Aztar in all the land." Zarf held his hands out in front of him then, rubbing his fingers and mumbling, "zweeee daw…" With that there was a small poof sound, and two small logs appeared, which Zarf gestured at. "Sit down, Travis."

Travis did as he was told, and Zarf began to explain all about his journey to the land of the sun.

"Netherless land is heading for hard times, as the Aztars try to enforce their dark magic upon the Glebbilins. On the day after Murtic stole the Stones, and as the sunlight had just begun to fade, I finished working on the time spell which was going to allow me to go back to the previous day to stop Murtic from stealing the great stones of Zar, when it all went wrong – I was too late. Murtic had banished the stones to another world and time at the precise moment I was creating a doorway to the past with my own spell."

After a brief pause, Zarf clapped his hands and shouted, "Bang! Now, this is where I've ended up, by an explosion of two powerful spells." He shrugged. "I seem to be in another dimension along with my own, as when the two spells collided it not only opened the gateway to another world and time, but it also split the two worlds alongside each other, and now I have the ability to pass between the two." He stared at the boy in front of him. "I need your help, Travis. I need to find the Stones and return with them to Netherless so I can free the Glebbilins from the Aztar, as well as from the dark magic forces at work that are slowly overcoming the Glebbilins and their peaceful existence."

-Travis-

I don't know how I can help," replied Travis sadly. "I've only just moved in today; I haven't even seen the inside of the house yet!"

"I have," replied Zarf knowingly, "and I can tell you that this is a very special house, with secret chambers and passageways, and many hidden secrets that were created when the two spells collided. This is why I need you to help me with my quest, I believe that you were chosen and this was not an accident for us to meet like this. Please! I have but only seven plays until the dark magic is irreversible," he pleaded.

"Seven plays? What do you mean by seven plays?" Travis asked.

"Time of the sun is when all play, time of the moon is when all sleep, but I have used up two plays already, so we have only five left."

"Where do you live now?" Travis asked, still unsure of what to make of all this. "Where do you sleep and what do you eat?"

"I live over there," Zarf replied, pointing over to a rock on the ground, right next to the huge tree. "I eat the red fruit from that tree, and the pointy things that go into the ground with little bushes on, and I also enjoy the variety of juicy whomps your garden has to offer."

Travis paused for a moment "What is a whomp?" He asked scratching the side of his head. "A whomp is a whomp, what else would a whomp be but a skinny whomp, fat whomp, juicy whomp any kind of whomp!" Staring down at the ground looking quite annoyed, Zarf suddenly looked up at Travis frowned and shouted. "It is just a whomp silly boy!" Pointing down to a long fat Wrigley worm quickly squirming and slithering its way back down a wet and slimy hole.

"Aah! You mean a worm?" Travis said with a disgusted look upon his face."

"Never mind you that, the translation will be muddled with a few words but not many, worm, whomp they all taste the same." Zarf replied with a puzzled look upon his thin and wrinkled face.

"I'll bring you some food and something to drink later; I best be heading back before my parents start worrying where I am

– they might come looking for me and find you too."

"Don't you worry about me; they cannot see me – only you can."

Travis nodded. "I had better go, Zarf, but I'll be back later with food and drink that I promised. I'll meet you at the rock when the sun goes down."

After saying goodbye to his new found friend, Travis walked back up to the house, thinking about everything Zarf had said. Was it true? Could it all be real?

He sure hoped so.

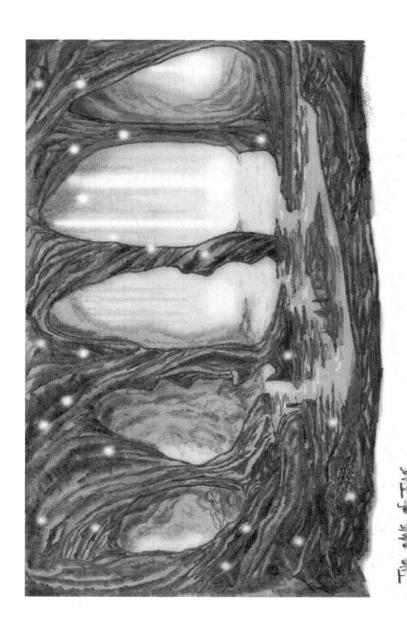

Walking up the steps at the back of the house – which led Travis to the back door, was the entrance to the kitchen.

He Pulled down on the door handle and entered as he made his way through to the main hallway. He wanted to find himself a bedroom – and to make sure it was not only a good one, but the best. Travis paused for just a few seconds before taking another step, as he stared his journey up the grand sweeping staircase which seemed to go on forever with no ending.

There were seven bedrooms on the first floor, but upon closer inspection, none of them looked out onto the back garden, which just wouldn't do – Travis needed to be able to see the mulberry tree from his bedroom window. Following the upstairs hallway to the very end, he came across another flight of stairs that led up towards the roof.

"This must lead to the attic," Travis mumbled to himself as he began climbing, and halfway up, he paused. There was another landing – a narrow one with a door at the end – so Travis decided to step onto the landing and walk towards it. As Travis turned the door's handle, it opened with a long, low creak, and there inside was the perfect room; not only did it look out over the back garden, but it also had a full view of the mulberry tree.

"Wow, this is great!" Travis said out loud to the empty room, suddenly excited. It was such a big room, but that wasn't what had caught Travis's attention; there was a huge twirly whirly slide that went right down through the floor into the room below. Travis peered over the edge – it looked dark down there, but that didn't stop him from wanting to try it out. He decided he'd give it a go once he'd settled and unpacked.

Still curious, Travis headed to the attic to see what was up there, and the first thing he noticed was just how huge it was – the attic stretched from one side of the house all the way across to the other – but that wasn't all: it was cold and musty and full of cobwebs, with ancient-looking furniture and many, many other things that had been hidden and forgotten about. Whereas other people might have looked at the attic and seen a pile of junk, Travis saw it as a treasure trove – he couldn't wait to start rifling through everything. He smiled to himself as he exclaimed, "What a day!" With that, he went downstairs to find his boxes, wanting to unpack everything as soon as possible.

**

Travis had spent the last three and a half hours cleaning and sorting out his new bedroom, and things were now more or less where he wanted them.

"Perfect!" he said to himself. "Now I need to find another torch and my backpack – then I can see where this slide leads to."

Travis went downstairs and headed to the kitchen, which was empty. After making sure no one was around, he made some peanut butter and strawberry jam sandwiches, grabbed two apples and two bananas, and filled up two bottles with water from the tap. He also sneaked a large packet of biscuits from the cookie cupboard before hiding the whole lot around the corner by the stairs. Satisfied they were hidden well enough and out of sight; he went to find his mom.

"Mom, is it alright if I stay in my room for the rest of the day?" Travis asked his mother. "I want to sort out the mess. I'll take a bath and go to sleep later when I get tired."

"Sure Travis," his mom replied, smiling at him. "It's been a long day, I know, and your father won't be back from work until later this evening." She shrugged. "It's the school holidays so do as you please; you know where I am if you need anything."

"Thanks Mom," Travis said, throwing her a quick smile before collecting his supplies and heading upstairs to his bedroom.

Closing the door behind him, Travis crept over to the slide. He then switched on one of the torches, letting it go down the slide and watching as it lit up the surrounding area. It went on for quite some time before coming to a stop, but Travis could just about see it below. "That's a long way down," Travis said, switching on the other torch and hopping onto the slide as he slung his backpack over his shoulders. "Here goes nothiiiiiiinggggg!" he shouted as he let go of the sides.

And then down Travis went, faster and faster, as the light from his torch grew closer with every twist and turn. He thought that at the speed he was going he'd never be able to stop himself, but as he neared the end of the slide, he found himself slowing down, eventually coming to a stop right at the very edge of the slide. He was clearly underground, the darkness around him making him shiver.

Grabbing hold of the torch he'd thrown down the slide,

Travis switched it off and tucked it under his shirt so he'd have a spare. He then stood up, dusted himself off, and headed off into the gloom, towards what sounded like someone munching and slurping.

Travis walked very carefully along the underground path – unsure of what he would encounter – and was more than a little surprised when he turned the corner to find Zarf standing in front of him, a bunch of carrots in one hand and a clenched fist full of worms in the other.

"Hello there!" Travis said, shining the torch on Zarf. His new found friend got such a fright, however, that he dropped the carrots and worms and disappeared in the blink of an eye.

"Zarf, it's me, Travis! Don't be afraid!" he called out.

"Afraid? Do I look afraid?" answered Zarf, his voice shaking slightly. "I just went to get my drink."

"Oh, is that why you dropped your carrots and earthworms?" Travis asked, with a hint of a smirk on his face.

Quickly changing the subject, Zarf replied, "So that's what these are: carrots and earthworms! Mmm, I like earthworms." He looked up at Travis. "So, you found the secret room with the slide then?"

"Yes," said Travis, nodding, "but it's not much of a secret room, being situated on the way up to the attic – there's nothing secretive about that now, is there? I found it straight away!" He raised his eyebrows at Zarf.

"Well, actually, there *is* a secret within the slide… you see, only you can use it," Zarf explained. "When you go down the slide, you end up all the way down here, but if anyone else were to use it, it would only take them to the ground floor's laundry room. But anyway, why did you come down here? How did you know it would lead you to me?"

"I didn't," Travis admitted. "I was just feeling inquisitive and thought I would investigate." He shrugged.

"Foolish boy," Zarf muttered, before ordering, "follow me!" He then headed towards the edge of the underground tunnel, and Travis followed as he continued on to a crevasse in the wall. He watched in amazement as Zarf walked through it.

"Well come along, what are you waiting for?" Zarf shouted from beyond the crevasse.

"I'll never fit through there!" Travis replied, a little panicked.

"Have you still no faith in the power of my magic?" Zarf asked. "Walk on through!"

Taking a deep breath, Travis walked through the gap, his body tensed as if he was just about to jump into an ice-cold swimming pool. After a second, he realised he'd passed through. "Cool, how do you do that stuff?" Travis asked Zarf, astonished.

"Time will tell, time will tell!" Zarf muttered, before adding brightly, "This is my home!"

"Holy cow, this place is huge!" Travis exclaimed, his face lighting up. "This is amazing; it's like a whole city underground, it even has a night sky with stars!" a little confused Travis got down on his stomach and used hie elbows to shimmer closer nearer to the edge to get a good look at what was below.

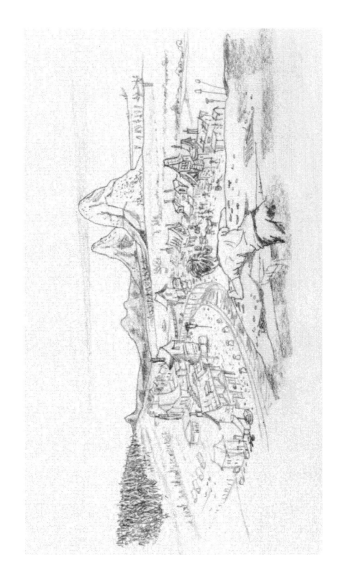

-Netherless Land-

"Welcome to Netherless," Zarf announced, before opening his mouth in a huge yawn. "We must rest now, as tomorrow we face a great journey to find the Stones of Zar."

Travis nodded. "Well, I'm hungry – don't worry, I've brought you some food too, Zarf," he said as he unclipped his backpack, pulling out the sandwiches, the biscuits, and the water.

"Here, try this – it's called a sandwich," Travis suggested as he held it out to Zarf.

Zarf took it from him, glancing at it suspiciously before taking a tentative bite. His eyes widened immediately, and he finished it off in an instant. In fact, he enjoyed the sandwich so much that he even ate Travis's other half. Travis then passed a cookie to Zarf.

"Mmm, this wood is tasty! Mmm, very tasty!" Zarf shouted.

"That's not wood; we call that a biscuit or a cookie, and we have many different types," he explained.

Zarf nodded enthusiastically. "I like cookies; do you have any more cookies, Travis?" he asked politely.

Travis gave Zarf more cookies, then watched as the little old Glebbilin made them instantly disappear – without the use of any magic what so ever.

Once they were full, they both sat for a few minutes, just gazing up at the sky over Netherless, when all of a sudden, they heard a whistling sound coming from beyond.

"What's that?" Travis asked Zarf.

"It's coming from your time," Zarf replied. "Let's go and take a look, and Travis – be careful," he warned.

So, with a deep breath and a last look at Netherless, Travis followed Zarf back through the crevasse – back to his world, his time.

-Zarf Eating a Cookie-

Holding his hands out in front of him, Zarf started rubbing his fingers and mumbling, "zweeee daw!" He then touched the rock that lay between the two walls, and poof! They were standing next to the huge mulberry tree in the garden.

"Wow, that was awesome!" Travis cried, before spotting his mother next to the house. "Hide, there's my mom!"

"Don't worry Travis," Zarf assured him. "When you're with me, you are in my time, so no one can see or hear you in your time unless you go back up the slide to your room – that is the doorway which separates the two worlds."

"Then how come I saw you this morning without having gone down the slide?" Travis asked, confused.

Zarf shook his head. "That's a mistake I won't be making again. Let's just say that I didn't know someone was going to be looking for a bird to shoot out of this tree for fun – which, I might add, is not a very kind thing to do." He shrugged. "I just thought I could get ten minutes of sunshine without using my magic; using magic in your world takes a lot out of a wizard."

"Ah! So, you're a wizard!" cried Travis, impressed. "I've read stories about wizards and sorcery... what kind of wizard are you?" he asked.

"I am known as the Great Zarf, keeper of the time stones – the Great Stones of Zar." He smiled proudly. "The stones have been in my possession from the beginning of time; I have to keep them safe from evil sorcerers and protect them from the dark magic..." He trailed off, sighing. "But I've failed my duties as a keeper, and now the Glebbilins of Netherless land are in trouble." He slumped down onto the ground with his head in his hands.

Travis and Zarf continued talking, having now completely forgotten about the whistling sound that had drawn them back to the surface in the first place.

"Zarf," said Travis, placing his hand on his friend's shoulder. "I want to help you and your people. Tell me all there is to know about the Stones and about your world, and tomorrow we must begin the quest to find these Great Stones and return them to their rightful place." He smiled at Zarf sympathetically.

"You will help Zarf – and his kind – restore order to the land of Netherless?" he asked, amazed.

"Yes, I will try my best to help," Travis confirmed, his mind now made up.

"Well then, we need to get started at time of moon," Zarf replied. "I will teach you some wizardry to help you in times of need."

Travis paused for a moment. "Time of moon is known as night-time and time of sun is known as daytime; I see now-just so we both know what we're talking about!" he explained.

Zarf nodded. "I got it: day and night. Now, Travis, you must go back up the slide and prepare – I will find you in your room at the time of moon… I mean, night-time. You must hurry; the moon is calling!"

Travis frowned. "But slides are for coming down, not going up!"

"I will show you; let's go back now," Zarf replied.

So, they both made their way back to the slide, and Zarf showed Travis how it would take him back up whenever he needed to return home; if he was to sit on the slide facing upwards, close his eyes, let go of the sides, and then open his eyes once again, Travis would slide right back to his room.

Picking up his backpack, Travis put his hands on the wizard's shoulders as he said, "I will be waiting for you, Zarf." Then he turned, and jumping onto the slide, he closed his eyes. As he'd been told, he let go of the sides, and when he opened his eyes again, he was already sliding upwards.

As he went, Travis heard a voice from behind crying out, "Cookies! Get more cookies!" It was Zarf, reminding Travis just how much he loved the biscuits. Travis laughed to himself as he entered his bedroom.

Hopping off the slide, Travis threw his backpack on the floor and then jumped onto his bed, lying face down on his pillow. After a few seconds he turned himself over, putting his hands behind his head as he looked up at the ceiling and said to himself, "I'm going to love this new house!" With that, he promptly fell asleep.

Not long after, however, Travis heard a voice calling out his name, bringing him up from the depths of sleep. "Travis! Travis, where are you?" It was his mother's voice. "Your supper's ready! I've been calling you for ages; your food's most probably gone cold by now!"

"I'm in my room – the one between the first floor and the attic!" Travis shouted back.

There was a slight pause. "What are you doing up there when there are so many other bedrooms to choose from down here?" she asked.

"I like it up here; this is the best room in the house. If it's OK, I want to make this my room," Travis explained.

Now rather intrigued, Travis's mother made her way up to his bedroom to take a look, and standing in the doorway, she let her eyes roam over the space, a small smile on her lips. "This is a lovely room for a boy of your age. How did you find it?" she asked. "I had no idea it was here!"

Travis shrugged. "Just lucky I guess."

Before he could say anything else, his mother interrupted: "Right, well I'm going to bed early tonight – it's been a long day and I have to get up early tomorrow morning to head into town. Please go downstairs and eat your supper." She smiled at her son. "I'll speak with you tomorrow. Goodnight, Travis."

"Goodnight, Mom," Travis replied.

Doing as he was told, Travis rushed downstairs and ate up all his supper before going to get some more food for his journey with Zarf the next morning. He took four packets of biscuits, four bottles of cola, six packets of crisps, two packs of Wine Gums, two chocolate bars, another two apples, and some dry bread. "This ought to be enough," Travis said, eyeing up his food haul and trying to reassure himself. He then went back upstairs, going through his drawers and cupboards and packing anything he thought he might need.

Once he was finished, Travis sat down on his bed, waiting eagerly for Zarf's visit.

He waited and he waited. An hour passed; it was getting late. Travis knew something was wrong – he could just feel it.

"I need to go; Zarf needs my help!" Travis thought to himself. "It's been far too long," he added in a nervous voice as he looked at his watch.

So, with his mind made up, he flung his backpack over his shoulders, grabbed the torch, and down the slide he went.

MULBERRY TREE

CHAPTER TWO

PATHFINDER

Travis headed towards the crevasse in the wall of the underground tunnel and walked through to Netherless land. As before, it was a spectacular sight: he looked out as if he were standing on a high mountain, staring out across the range. He could see hundreds of little lights flickering in the distance as the trees swayed to and fro with the warm breeze the night had to offer, and upon looking down the side of the mountain, he was quite taken aback with the height.

"What am I going to do?" he asked himself. "How am I going to get down this mountain?"

Just then, however, he heard a noise: it sounded like whistling, and after pausing to listen to it for a moment, he realised it was coming from under the ground on which he stood. Intrigued, Travis started to slowly follow the whistling sound, but after he'd gone only 15 metres or so, it stopped. His eyes widened as he saw what looked like a green light of some kind shining from a small hole in the ground.

Whipping off his backpack, Travis started rummaging through its contents until he found what he was looking for. "Yes!" he exclaimed as he pulled out a dessert spoon and started digging up the ground, "This has to be of importance, otherwise it wouldn't have lured me in its direction." He paused for a moment, looking at the light. "On the other hand, it could be a trick to get me over here." He shrugged. "I suppose I'll just have to take the chance and go with my instincts."

Travis continued digging up the dirt with his spoon, and although it took a good 15 minutes to widen the hole enough for him to reach down and try grabbing the shining object, it was no use; he just couldn't get a good grip on it.

Still, he was determined to get to the bottom of this, so Travis continued digging. After a while – and by now he was getting quite tired – a bright green light burst through the ground, illuminating everything in sight.

Travis looked up at the light in awe, but then something else occurred to him: the appearance of the light was announcing his presence to everyone in this strange land, so, in a panic, he shoved his hand as hard as he could into the hole, grabbing what felt like an ice-cold rock and pulling it out, making sure to keep it well covered with both of his hands so the light wouldn't spill out. Then, as fast as he could, he headed back through the crevasse in the wall, moving from Netherless land to his own world.

Once Travis was back on familiar ground, he felt safe, and kneeling down, he put the shining green rock on the floor. He watched as the glow became weaker and dimmer, the astonishing light petering out until it looked like a small green marble – almost like the jewels his mother had on her bracelets. "That's it!" Travis shouted with joy, looking down at the small object. "This must be one of the stones Zarf was telling me about! It has to be… but I don't understand why it was still in Netherless land," he mumbled to himself. Something wasn't quite adding up here.

As he bent over and picked up the stone for a closer look, it started to shine once again, though not quite as brightly as it had done before.

Travis was just holding the stone up in the air for a closer inspection when all of a sudden, he heard voices coming from behind the crevasse in the wall. Quickly putting the stone in his pocket, he walked over to the wall and put his ear up against it. He couldn't hear anything clearly, and he knew that he couldn't take the chance of walking back through the crevasse in case he got spotted by some evil wizard. "If only I knew where Zarf was," he thought to himself, "he'd know what to do with this stone."

Travis wondered what he should do, going over his options in his mind. He could run through quickly, or perhaps just put his head through the crevasse, or maybe even just an arm, just to see what would happen…

"That's it!" he said to himself after a few moments. "I'll wait until it's quiet and then I'll just put my head through." With his mind made up, Travis sat with his back up against the wall, waiting for all to become quiet on the other side.

He waited and he waited, and about an hour later, Travis could hear no other noise apart from the low, rumbling sound of someone snoring. He decided that the time had come – he would pop his head through the crevasse and take a quick look. So, without wasting another second, Travis started to ease his head through the crevasse, though he did it with extreme caution. He could feel a cold breeze blowing on his nose – the first part of his body to penetrate the crevasse – and then he put the rest of his face through the gap in the wall.

"Great spaghetti!" he exclaimed to himself, before quickly withdrawing his head from the crevasse. "Who are these creatures?!"

-Trogg Accepting the Button-

Still trying to get over his surprise, Travis slumped down against the wall and immediately started plotting his plan of action. He thought back to what he'd seen: six little creatures that looked like goblins of some sort had been standing with their backs to him. They'd been looking out over the land of Netherless as one lay asleep against the wall. The sleeping goblin had rather resembled Zarf, though perhaps he was a little thinner.

Quickly, Travis stood up and popped his head through the crevasse once again, but this time he stayed standing like that a little longer than he had before. He took a good look around the area, taking everything in in great detail before pulling back.

Travis thought for another moment, realising that the one laying against the crevasse – the one that resembled Zarf – must in fact be Murtic, the evillest Glebbilin turned Aztar in the land. He also thought that the other six must be Aztars too; it seemed like they were keeping watch while Murtic had a nap, looking out for their leader.

While Travis was working out the situation, another significant detail came flooding back to him: Murtic had been holding something in his hand – a vibrant purple stone. "That must be one of the stones," Travis said to himself. "I don't know how many stones there are in total, but I have to get that one from Murtic!" So, popping his head and his hand slowly and quietly through the crevasse, he reached down over Murtic to try and grab hold of the stone.

Just as Travis put his fingers around the stone, Murtic grunted and snorted, turning further away from Travis and closing his hand more tightly around the stone. Travis pulled away as fast as he could, disappearing back into the crevasse.

Travis listened from the other side of the wall as Murtic cried out in an angry voice, "What was that?! Why was no one watching? Something or someone has just been here! Right next to me!"

"No, your greatness, we have been keeping watch and nothing could or has passed by," one of the Aztar replied.

Murtic, however, wasn't having any of it. "I felt the presence of another wizard – he or she is here! I want you to find the wizard and bring him or her to me so I can banish them – along with Zarf – to another time!"

At this point, Travis risked poking his face through the crevasse again – but only a little. He simply had to know what was going on.

He watched as Murtic held out the purple rock in his bony little hand, pointing it at the Aztar that had answered him back. As he did so, he began saying out loud, "Azar-atar-aztar!" The rock lit up brightly and a beam of purple light focused on the Aztar, who fell to his knees and cupped his hands together in front of him.

"No, your greatness, not me!" he shouted. "Not Trogg, master, pleeeeease!" This was all that could be heard before he was banished to another time and place.

"Let that be a lesson to all of you!" Murtic warned them, a hint of menace in his voice. "If any of you decide to defy me, that's what will happen! Now find me that wizard, and fetch Zarf and bring him to me!" he shouted.

Travis pulled back from the crevasse before Murtic or anyone else could notice him, leaning against the wall as he gathered his thoughts. "They're going to capture Zarf... I need to find out more! I also need to get to the other side without being seen, but how?" he asked himself as he tried to devise a plan. Not only did he need to find the Great Stones of Zar, but he also had to free Zarf as well.

Just then, Travis noticed a green light starting to shine brighter and brighter from the inside of his pocket. "The stone," he mumbled to himself, putting his hand into his pocket and pulling it out. "I remember now; the stones have the power to protect from evil and dark magic! But how? And how many stones are there?" Travis didn't know, but he *did* know that he'd have to find Zarf to find out more.

As Travis opened his hand, the stone shone brightly in his palm, and the more Travis stared at the bright green light, the more he was beginning to be pulled into a deep trance. Soon it became clear that the stone was feeding Travis information by showing him visions of the Glebbilins, the Aztars, and the Netherless lands.

The light grew dim as Travis fell to the ground, unconscious and weak, still clutching the stone. Unbeknown to him, Travis had been chosen to have the mystical powers of the Great Stones bestowed upon him, and the knowledge to understand the way of the Glebbilins and their world.

Travis had been unconscious for about an hour when he heard a voice calling out to him.

"Travis… Travis… Travis, wake up!" the voice called out in a gentle tone.

Travis opened his eyes – but slowly, as if they had been stuck down with honey – and as he tried to focus his vision on the blurry image standing over him, he jumped to his feet. "Who are you?" Travis demanded. "How long have I been asleep for? What happened to me?" He paused for a moment, putting his hands over his face. "Aargh, my head!"

"Sit down for a while and regain your strength," the person – who wasn't really a person, as he was tiny – told Travis, smiling at him. "My name is Orgus and I am a friend of the great Zarf – he told me how to find you. He also asked me to give you this." Orgus held out his small little hand, and resting in his tiny palm was a tiny book, just 1.5 cm in length by 1 cm in width.

The little book didn't seem too out of place, however, as Orgus himself only stood about 20 cm high, meaning that he had the smallest little hands you could ever imagine.

What am I supposed to do with this tiny little book?" Travis asked. "The words will be far too small for me to read!"

"This is a very special book – a very powerful book – and you have been chosen to receive it," Orgus replied, falling to his knees and clutching at Travis's leg dramatically. "You are the Chosen One, Sir, just as the ancient markings have shown us on every wall of the Cave of Time. You are the Chosen One, the one from beyond, the one who is to be part of the Stones of Zar," Orgus added, gazing at Travis with a strange kind of admiration.

"I still can't read the book, Orgus," Travis replied, a little bewildered by the whole thing.

"Oh Sir, you don't *read* the book; you have to place it on your tongue and then repeat after me," Orgus explained.

"What happens then?" Travis asked, now very much intrigued.

-Murtic-

"You will absorb all the knowledge and wisdom surrounding the Glebbilins' magic for the past several centuries, Sir, and you will then be a pathfinder, Sir, and choose the passages to travel, Sir," Orgus replied, as if that cleared up everything. "Now, place the book on your tongue and repeat after me," he pleaded with Travis, staring at him with wide eyes.

So, not knowing what else to do, Travis placed the tiny little book on his tongue and then waited for his commands.

"Marideea – magica – marideea – magica – magica – majith!" Orgus spoke out loud.

Travis took a deep breath and repeated, "Marideea magica – marideea – magica – magica majith!" He looked around him, waiting, but when nothing happened, he took another deep breath and repeated the same words, but this time with pauses in between each of them, just as Orgus had spoken them. "Marideea – magica – marideea – magica – magica – majith!"

Just then, Travis felt all light-headed and dizzy, and the next moment he fell to his knees, once again putting his hands over his ears to cover them as he started mumbling to himself.

Orgus grinned, lifting his arms as if to flap them like wings, and with a quick nod at Travis – who wasn't really paying any attention to him – he morphed into a bird and flew away.

Travis had been in a trance for more than twenty minutes, and since his last contact with Zarf – which was well over six hours ago – Travis had now been inducted as the pathfinder, the Selector of travel and time. He was now a fully-fledged wizard, as he possessed all the Glebbilins' knowledge, along with every great wizard spell ever known to the Glebbilins of Netherless land.

Travis was the first wizard pathfinder, and while being a wizard (or just a pathfinder) is difficult enough, being a time travelling wizard is incredibly hard to get your head around. As Travis was the Chosen One, he had to use his new found skills for good use – and *only* good use.

So, the time had now come for Travis to begin his journey, to free Zarf and to find and return the Stones of Zar.

Now bursting with knowledge that had come to him during his trance, Travis started whispering to himself: "Six stones in total… the sequence stones are red, blue, orange, and yellow, and without these four, the stones cannot function properly… there's green which is the stone to free one from time, and that means that the green stone allows you to find your way back, and is a positive stone that wards of all negativity and evil… then there's the purple stone that bends time, which allows you to move forwards. It is a negative stone and one that welcomes negativity and evil."

He paused, thinking to himself for a moment before continuing. "I have the green stone, which allows me to return, but if I haven't gone anywhere, I can't return and I can't go anywhere unless I have the purple stone that Murtic has, and that is why he is able to banish whatever and whoever he likes to other places… but without the other four stones he cannot choose their destination; he doesn't even know where they go. The green stone remained hidden in Netherless land because it must have known there was dark wizardry at play, as Murtic kept the purple stone to increase his own magic powers and banish the other stones…"

He paced up and down, scratching his chin as he carried on. "I need to get that purple stone from Murtic, and then I can track down the other four stones which lie in their chosen destiny – that would be North for the blue stone, South for the red stone, East for the orange stone, and West for the yellow stone. The purple stone is the passage way to the destination and the green stone is the passage way back, all fitting together like a compass. So… I've got it! I just have to put all the stones together, which will then become my pathfinder!" With this realisation, Travis started jumping around excitedly – he knew that he now had all the answers, and more importantly, he had the upper hand on Murtic! He just had to find Zarf and get the purple stone from Murtic.

One and a half hours had passed since Travis had heard Murtic instruct the Aztar to get Zarf, and Travis knew Murtic was going to banish him by using the purple stone – Travis just hoped Murtic was still searching for him.

Reaching down into his bag, he pulled out some black string, which he then used to tie the green stone up in a spider web type of pattern. He then tied it around his neck as if it were a necklace, before popping it down his shirt so that it was concealed from everyone. He stood up, fastened his backpack, and headed towards the crevasse, where he slowly popped his head through. After a quick look around, he realised there was nobody in sight, so he slowly edged his way through to the other side. He was now in Netherless land.

-Muftish-

-Mulisty-

CHAPTER THREE

TRIP THROUGH TIME

All was still and quiet way up above the land of Netherless. All that could be heard was the sound of insects calling to one another, and all that could be seen was the flickering lights of the little insects as they tried to communicate with each other in the darkness. Yes, everything was quiet where Travis was standing, up on the hill overlooking Netherless land… in fact, it seemed a little too quiet.

With only five days left to reunite the stones and free the Glebbilins, Travis had to act quickly to find Zarf and get the purple stone from Murtic to complete his quest.

A rustling sound in the tree to his right caught Travis's attention, and he walked over to investigate. Looking up, he said, "Hello! Is there anyone there?" In response, he heard yet more rustling, and from nowhere three little Aztars leapt out of the tree and flung a net over his head, capturing him.

The three Aztars danced around with joy as they mocked, "We have the wizard, the little, little wizard! We shall lock him up with Zarf until Murtic returns at the time of play!"

"If you're not careful I'll turn you all into mushrooms and then gobble you up!" Travis shouted, remembering how Zarf had warned him with the same threat the first time they'd met.

The Aztars stared at Travis before turning to each other. "How does he know about that?"

Realising that he was rattling them, Travis pointed to the Aztars and started saying any old words he could think of: "Hoil, coil, mushroom…"

"No, stop!" one of the Aztars begged Travis. "We won't hurt you! Please don't turn us into mushrooms; we don't taste very good, honest!"

"Why not?" asked Travis. "You were going to hand me to Murtic so I could be banished from Netherless land, weren't you? And where is my student, Zarf?"

"Zarf is your student?" one of the Aztar – Zeed – asked.

"Yes, he is," Travis replied, staring at them with what he hoped was a look of power and strength.

With that, they all fell to their knees as Zeed said, "Oh, powerful one, please, we didn't know you were the teacher of Zarf! Oh, powerful one, fear not: we will take you to Zarf."

The three Aztar – Zeed, Muftish, and Mulisty – turned to face the big tree. They pointed at it, and with a click of their fingers, the trunk opened. Travis could see Zarf slowly emerging from within.

"Zarf, you're alright!" Travis shouted, unable to hide his obvious happiness. His friend nodded to him.

"Oh, powerful one, please release us!" Zeed begged.

Travis looked at him for a second, as though considering his request. "I'm not sure that would be such a good idea," he said eventually.

"Ooooh," said the Aztars unhappily as they handed Zarf to Travis.

Travis welcomed Zarf back and asked if everything was OK.

"All is well for now, oh master," Zarf said, looking at Travis and winking at him. "Maybe we should turn them into little bushes so they can be stepped upon whenever someone walks up here?" he asked, a mischievous glint in his eye.

"No," replied Travis, "I think we should let them go back to Murtic, as long as they take him this message: let him know that the great wizard Travis has arrived, that he's freed Zarf, and that he is now waiting for Murtic."

And with that, Zeed, Muftish, and Mulisty turned and ran down the path along the side of the mountain as fast as their little feet would carry them.

"What have you done, Travis?" Zarf asked in a state of panic, his jokey demeanour now completely gone. "Murtic has the purple stone, and with that stone in his possession, he is extremely powerful."

"Relax, Zarf," Travis replied calmly, "they think I'm as powerful as you are, and even more powerful than Murtic after I told them I was your teacher – and after I threatened to turn them into mushrooms."

Zarf breathed a sigh of relief. "I'm glad you came back to rescue me, thank you. Did Orgus meet up with you?"

"Yes, he did," Travis replied, before going on to tell Zarf everything that had happened since they'd last been together.

"You have the green stone?" Zarf asked. "Why didn't you tell me this earlier?"

Travis shrugged. "I thought, seeing as you're a wizard and all, you would have known."

"Yes, a wizard, not a mind reader… although that would be great if I could read minds," Zarf pondered, "because then I could…"

"That's enough, Zarf," Travis said. "We don't need to hear about all that now; we need to get to work! Here's my plan: we need to be banished by Murtic, because whatever he banishes can only go along one path. All the stones are out of place and there is only one destination, so wherever Trogg has been sent, that is where we will find the four missing stones. Once we have the stones, we can find Trogg and then find our way back with the green stone." Travis smiled. "Murtic has no idea that I have the green stone – he thinks it's been banished with the other four."

Zarf nodded. Travis had it all worked out, and now all he and Zarf needed to do was wait for Murtic to return so he could banish the two of them from Netherless land.

Back at Murtic's, the three Aztars were telling the story (stretching the truth just a little) of how this mighty and powerful wizard had turned them into trees and had freed Zarf, and of how they'd had to use their own cunningness to get Travis to turn them back again, so they could escape to warn Murtic about the danger of this powerful wizard who goes by the name, Travis.

Murtic laughed as they told their story, the other two Aztars –Treap and Woizle – joining in.

"What are you two laughing at?" Murtic shouted suddenly, pulling out his purple stone and pointing it at them.

They shook and clung to one other in fear. "Please, your greatness; you need us to capture this new wizard so you can banish him from Netherless land!" the two said with smiles on their faces.

Murtic thought for a moment. "You're right, this time round.... I have the purple stone, and no one can stop me now, ha ha ha haaa!" With that, he threw his cloak over his shoulders and headed for the door, summoning the five Aztars to follow and then commanding them to take the lead.

They made their way outside to where a sheet of wood was standing up against the wall, pausing as Murtic pointed to the sheet. It slid down onto the floor in front of them.

"Hop on!" he yelled. Murtic then made all six of them rise above the village and head up towards the mountains.

Travis looked up at the sky. "Zarf, I can see something approaching in the distance... what could it be?"

"That would be Murtic on his travels to meet you," Zarf

replied, squinting up at the sky. "I'd get ready now, if I were you."

Murtic – along with his five companions – landed very gently, and as soon as they were on solid ground, all five of the Aztars jumped off and ran to cower behind Murtic, leaving him to confront Travis and Zarf.

"Get back here, you slithering cowards!" Murtic demanded, watching as they all moved forward – three on the left and two on the right of Murtic. They mumbled, "Yes, your greatness, sorry, your greatness, won't do that again, your greatness," as they went.

"So, you are the wizard Travis, the mighty and powerful Travis, ha ha ha haaa!" Murtic laughed. "You are no more than a mere boy from a parallel world; I know of your kind. I knew it as soon as I heard the name T.R.A.V.I.S – your kind don't even do magic; I've been there, so I know this. You might have fooled the three Aztars, but you can't fool me – I'm half Aztar half Glebbilin." Murtic held the purple rock in his bony little hand, and as he pointed it at Travis and Zarf, he began saying out loud, "Azar-atar-aztar!"

Upon hearing those words, all the Aztars covered their eyes, unable to watch. They feared that Murtic was going to be banished by the mighty wizard Travis for speaking to him in such a manner.

The rock lit up brightly and a beam of purple light shone out of it, quickly splitting into two as it focused on both Travis and Zarf.

Travis and Zarf stared at Murtic as Travis said out loud for all to hear: "I will return in four days with Trogg, and those who choose not to follow me shall feel my P – O – W –E–R!" And with that, they were banished from Netherless land.

Murtic spun around, causing his cloak to ripple in the air as he held his hands up high. "You see, I am the greatest! I am Murtic the Great!" He grinned at the Aztars in front of him.

In a rather shaky and scared voice, Zeed asked Murtic, "But they said they'd be back in four days… what if this is true, your greatness?"

"I don't want to hear it!" he spat. "They can never return; do I make myself clear? I am Murtic the Great!"

"Yes, master, yes, your greatness," the Aztar repeated over and over as they stepped back onto the sheet of wood that would take them back down the mountain. They didn't dare say anything else about the great wizard Travis.

Once back inside his home – which was little more than a hut – Murtic called all the Aztars to a meeting, where he told them what was going to happen in a few days' time.

"I, Murtic, will rule Netherless land as soon as the dark magic forces are at play and have overcome the Glebbilins, turning their peaceful existence into havoc!" He grinned again, something that caused more than one of the Aztars to slowly back away from him.

While Murtic was thinking about ruling Netherless land, Travis and Zarf were just entering the land to which they'd been banished.

They both looked around, wondering where they could be, and although it was dark, it wasn't too dark to see their surroundings. The land looked similar to Netherless land, but there was a strange atmosphere about the place that Travis couldn't quite put his finger on.

-Orgus-

After a few moments of silence, Travis looked at Zarf and asked, "Why did you not use your magic back in Netherless land?"

"One cannot use great magic in Netherless land unless you are a keeper of the Stones of Zar," Zarf explained, "and I lost that privilege when I failed my duties as a Keeper." He sighed. "But if you are not a keeper and manage to have the purple stone, you can use any magic in Netherless land. Murtic knew that."

"But I have the green stone and all the knowledge of wizardry; do you think I can perform magic spells?" Travis asked, getting excited at the thought.

"No, you need to harness the power first and use it wisely," Zarf replied.

"But I've been chosen and I understand the power, so how will I know when I'm ready?" Travis asked, already feeling a little disappointed.

"Travis, you are a wizard, but not just any wizard – you are a pathfinder," Zarf explained. "This was your destiny, just like the others before you and the others like yourself in other worlds. You must not hurry magic; it will come to you when the time is right." Travis opened his mouth to speak, but Zarf held up his hand to stop him. "You will know when the time is right, Travis, you will know. Don't worry." He smiled, trying to comfort his friend, before walking away.

Travis looked around him, spotting what appeared to be a tree house of some sort about 100 metres away. He walked over to Zarf, who was now sitting on the ground with his face lowered into his hands. Crouching down, he patted Zarf on the back and said, "Zarf, look, I can see some type of tree house in the distance! I have a bag full of food and drink, and we can use the tree house to rest up – it's really late, and we need our energy for tomorrow; it will be the countdown from day five until all in Netherless land is irreversible."

Suddenly thinking of something, Zarf jumped up, looking at Travis with a beaming smile. "Do you have any cookies in your bag?"

"Ah yes," Travis replied, smiling. "I brought some cookies especially for you, Zarf."

Zarf clapped his hands in excitement as they both headed towards the tree house.

It didn't take long for them to get to the enormous tree, and when they did, they looked up at it in awe. There was a big house built right in the centre amongst the branches and leaves, with an old tattered rope dangling down from it.

The only problem was, the rope didn't reach the ground, and neither Travis nor Zarf could see anything around that would help them reach the tree house.

After thinking for a moment, Travis held out his hands and started mumbling, "Abu – geera!" but nothing happened. After repeating the words several times, still there was nothing happening, and Travis turned to Zarf in exasperation. "That's it, I need something to harness the magic and power and to channel it in the right direction… something like a wand or pointer even just a straight stick."

Travis looked around; he and Zarf were surrounded by sticks that had fallen from the tree, and after searching through the sticks for several minutes, Travis had narrowed his selection down to just three – he wanted the perfect stick that he could use to aid his magic, and the straighter the better.

"Now, which one should I use?" he asked himself as he pushed all three sticks into the ground. "The one with the least bend would be the strongest; that would be the one to choose, wouldn't it?" he asked Zarf.

The decision made, Travis released the two bendy sticks and held the strongest of the three in his hand. Pointing the stick directly at the tattered and torn rope, he continued to mumble, "Abu – geera!" This time it worked, and after a split second, the torn rope was replaced by a sturdy-looking rope ladder.

"Wow, how did you know what to say, Travis?" asked Zarf, impressed.

"I don't know; it just flew out my mouth as if I'd known all along! It's amazing – I can do magic, Zarf!" he beamed.

"You are the Chosen One, Travis," said Zarf, nodding. "Just as I said earlier, you've been given a gift and your time has now come – it has come rather soon, but it is your time nevertheless – and you need to use this gift wisely, and only for the sake of good."

Travis agreed and then began the climb, with Zarf following at his heels. When Travis reached the top, he pulled himself onto the ledge before turning around and giving Zarf a hand up.

They slowly walked around the perimeter of the house before entering through the door, which was only accessible by climbing up another ladder on the side of the house and then down through a skylight on the roof. It was very well made, and incredibly sturdy – it was almost like a real house.

"What a place to have a door!" Zarf said.

"Well, I think it's quite clever," Travis replied, "because once you're inside, you pull up the ladder and there's no way of getting in. It's quite safe really!" Zarf nodded in agreement.

They both climbed down through the square skylight and into what looked like one big room. There were an amazing twenty-seven beds all lined up neat on the one side, with a long table on the other. At one end of the room there was a fireplace and at the other end there was a door.

"I wonder what's in that room, Zarf," Travis whispered, as he walked over and turned the knob, gently pushing the door open. "Ah, the shower and toilet; I should have known that." He looked around the little bathroom, impressed. He'd never been in a tree house with plumbing before!

They both walked over to where the beds were, trying each one of them to test for comfort, then Travis took off his backpack, put it behind his head, and lay down. Zarf also lay his head down, like a ton of bricks falling off a table, and they both fell asleep instantly.

It had been a very long day for both of them, and they needed to catch up on some well-deserved rest so they could think properly and plan ahead.

They both slept peacefully throughout the night – neither of them waking up even once – but were awoken by a loud bang in the early hours of the morning.

"What the… what was… who's there?" Travis asked in a trembling voice as he sat up in his bed. There was no answer. "Did you hear that, Zarf?" Travis asked, looking over at his friend.

"Yes, what was that?" Zarf replied with his own question.

"I don't know," Travis said, looking up at the roof. "Did we close that hatch yesterday after coming through?" he asked.

"No," replied Zarf, thinking back. "It was too hot in here so we left it open." He started to relax. "That's it, it was just the hatch slamming shut – I bet the wind picked up out there and caused it to fall down!"

Travis nodded, though he didn't look entirely convinced. "Well, we'd better get up and get ourselves cleaned! We need to start planning our next move."

And that is exactly what the pair of them did.

They both showered one after the other, then Travis put on some clean clothes while Zarf put his same clothes and robe back on. They then sat around the table as Travis started to undo his backpack, one clip at a time.

Zarf watched Travis impatiently, eventually shouting out,

"Come on, then! How difficult is it to undo a clip on a bag? Come on, hurry up!"

Amused at how exasperated Zarf was getting, Travis replied, "Wait a second; I'll have it open soon!" After opening his backpack, Travis reached into his bag and pulled out a pack of oat biscuits followed by two bottles of cola and some dry bread. "Are you hungry, Zarf?"

"What kind of question is that?" Zarf replied, leaning over the food to get a better look. "Are you hungry? Of course I'm hungry!"

"OK, there's no need to be ratty!" Travis said, laughing to himself.

"Ratty?" Zarf repeated. "Do I look like a rat to you?"

Travis shook his head. "No, where I come from it's just another way to say stop being miserable."

"Miserable? I'm not miserable! Although there *has* been

enough cause to be miserable," Zarf answered in an excited but rude way.

Travis shook his head again. "Right, here's a special drink that will give you loads of energy, and here are two slices of dry bread to fill up your tummy. You can also have these cookies to snack on. Now, I will halve the pack but you must save as much as you can, as we don't know how long we'll be here or if there's any food for us to eat around here, OK?"

Zarf reluctantly agreed, and they both began to sip their colas and pick at the dry bread.

After a few minutes, Travis asked Zarf the big question. "How was Murtic able to get hold of the Stones of Zar?"

Swallowing the bread, he'd been chewing on, Zarf began to explain what had happened on the Great Wott's celebration day.

"It was a day of fun and happiness in Netherless land as the Great Wott prepared for the celebration of his daughter's birthday," he started. "Everyone gathered near the Cave of Time where Jennith the Great Wott's daughter was receiving her place in Netherless land. All were partying and celebrating and having a great time. I decided to go over and congratulate Hop the Great Wott – only for a few seconds – and on my return to the Cave of Time, I found that the Stones of Zar had been stolen." He lowered his head in shame before carrying on with his story. "I immediately sounded the alarm and everyone started to panic – they all gathered their children and stood before the Great Wott to listen to what he had to say."

"What is a Wott anyway?" Travis interrupted. "And what was this celebration all about?"

"A Wott is one who advises and looks after the Glebbilins and the land," Zarf explained. "The celebration was about the Great Wott's daughter coming of age to make her own decisions in life, and to take her father's place one day as the Great Wott, should anything happen to him."

Travis thought this through. "So, he's kind of a king, and his daughter must have been celebrating becoming a teenager… I get it now; it all makes sense! So, what happened when they'd all gathered to hear Hop speak? What did he say, Zarf?"

"Well, he told everyone that this day was the beginning of what could be a long battle between good and evil in Netherless land. He told of how their great Zarf, keeper of the Stones, had let down his guard and that a pathfinder was the only one who could return the stones to their rightful place and restore harmony. Hop said it was within the stones that this was to take place and that now the time had come. I was ordered by the great Wott of Netherless land to find the pathfinder and to return the Great Stones of Zar, and that was when I left in shame; I went to search for a magic spell to bend time by just one day so I could try to stop the theft of the stones."

"So that was when you accidently created a doorway?" Travis asked, trying to keep up with the story.

"Yes," confirmed Zarf. "My spell was cast at the precise moment that Murtic opened a doorway himself – he wanted to banish the stones far away so nothing would foil his plans to fill the lands with evil. With all the stones banished except for the purple stone, Murtic knew he could rein havoc upon Netherless land, filling it with evil." Zarf shuddered slightly.

Travis stared into the distance, thinking. "That will never happen," he assured his friend. "I've been putting together this whole story, piece by piece, and it is my understanding that Murtic has no idea how the stones actually work. Just think about it: when he banished the stones, they didn't all just cling together and disappear into another time or place, because when he released the purple stone from the others, he altered their way of travel. The stones which stand for the four symbols of direction – North which is blue, South which is red, East which is orange, and West which is yellow – have no choice but to travel to those particular destinations as the purple stone and the green stone need to be part of that structured layout to aid in its travels. This is because the purple is the gateway to the exit and the green is the reopening of that gateway to return; you see, Zarf, without all the stones in place, there is a missing link, and if there is a missing link, each stone will become one on its own. This is what has happened." Travis shrugged, hoping he was explaining this properly.

Zarf nodded. "Go on, Travis; I'm listening."

"Well," he continued, "when you cast your spell and Murtic tried to banish the stones, both spells clashed and opened an invisible hole – the hole that has remained open for the purple stone to be used to send anything in its path through. You see, it opened and never closed again, thanks to your spell, so everything that Murtic banishes will end up here… it's just a matter of where. Murtic believes that he's scattering the banished items all over the place, but in fact the hole cannot be sealed until all the stones have been reunited. So, when Murtic banished the stones by removing the purple stone, the green stone could not follow as it worked hand in hand with the purple stone, so instead of it going with the other four stones, it remained hidden at the gateway's exit, while the other four stones were spread out and hidden in the four corners of this parallel world." He paused for a moment, remembering something. "I was fortunate to have heard the sound that drew me to find the green stone. Now, if we can locate the four stones we can travel back, as I have the green stone which is for returning. The power of all five stones together will be so strong that the purple stone will have no option but to be reunited with them, and then we just have to find out how they need to be placed – and where – in order for this action to take place." He finished, looking over at Zarf. "What do you think?"

Zarf nodded as he mulled everything over. "That all makes sense; it means that Trogg and the stones should be out there somewhere. The green stone found you, Travis, and this is no accident: you are the pathfinder, and this is your destiny."

"Murtic thinks he has the upper hand, but he's in for a surprise!" Travis Told Zarf, with a gleam in his eye.

Zarf didn't seem quite as enthusiastic as Travis, however.

"Murtic might well have the upper hand, Travis, if we don't return the stones to the Cave of Time within the time frame. Then, the dark magic will be irreversible and we will never be able to free the Glebbilins from the Aztars and the dark magic forces at work. As a result, the Glebbilins and their peaceful existence will be lost forever."

They both finished off their bread and cola in silence, thinking about what to do next. They each had a good understanding of what had happened, and what needed to happen to rectify the situation that had taken place at the hands of Murtic – the evillest Glebbilin-turned-Aztar.

Time was getting shorter.

-Zeed-

CHAPTER FOUR

WAY OF TROGG

Once they'd finished eating, Travis and Zarf continued to discuss their plans to defeat Murtic.

"So, we need to find Trogg," said Zarf, "and when we do, he'll be your server until you decide when to free him. You see, Travis, the Aztars have magic but are not allowed to use it while they are not free from their master; they are only allowed to use certain spells that aren't harmful to anyone."

"Is their magic powerful?" Travis asked, intrigued.

"Yes, but only if used with the master's permission and guidance," Zarf answered.

"What will happen if they decide to use it without permission?" Travis asked. Zarf shrugged as he casually replied, "They will turn into dust, as this spell was cast upon the Aztar long before time began. And before you ask me… no, I don't know the reason behind that dreadful spell."

"They must have done something really bad for that type of curse to be cast upon them," Travis mused to himself.

Getting up from their chairs, the two of them moved away from the table. Travis did a last check on his supplies before making sure everything in his backpack was in order for the trip.

"Right, we've got four apples, two bananas, two bottles of water, three packets of biscuits, two bottles of cola, six packets of crisps, two packs of Wine Gums, two chocolate bars, and some dry bread still left. There's also the compass my grandfather gave me, two torches, some marbles..." Travis quietly checking off all the items in his backpack, then he placed the compass on the table along with five different coloured marbles: blue, red, orange, yellow, and green.

"What are those things, Travis?" Zarf asked.

"This is a compass that will lead us to the stones by showing us the correct direction, and these are marbles – I'll use them as decoys if necessary." Travis put the marbles in his pocket and hung the compass around his neck.

"What is a decoy?" Zarf asked, bewildered.

"It means to distract somebody, or to deceive someone or divert their attention. We might need a distraction – you never know what might happen," he answered as he threw his backpack over his left shoulder.

"You have too many words for one meaning," Zarf said as he shook his head.

"I know," Travis said, bending down to tie his shoelaces with a double knot – he wanted to make sure they didn't come undone while he was exploring this new place. Once he was done, Travis picked up his magic stick and stuck it in his belt for quick access.

"Ready Zarf," he said, urging him over to the ladder. "Let's get going!" With that, they both went up the ladder and exited the tree house, ready for their adventure. After all, the five-day countdown had now begun, and they couldn't afford to waste any time.

As the pair began to climb down the rope ladder of the tree house, Zarf closed the hatch behind him, and once they'd reached ground level, Travis pulled out his magic stick.

Pointing at the ladder, he said the magic words (abu – geera) and watched in satisfaction as the ladder disappeared.

Turning to Zarf, Travis said, "This stick is now called my plinth. Nobody must know that it's a magic stick, and the more I use it, the more powerful it will become." Travis pushed the plinth between his belt and his trousers before holding up the compass and pointing to the right of where they were standing. "We'll go North to start with, working our way to each of the four corners until we have all four of the stones."

Zarf nodded in agreement, and the two of them set off in their chosen direction, which would lead them towards the mountains.

Half an hour into their walk, Zarf was starting to feel anxious. "We must act fast, Travis," he said, looking up at his friend. "Why do you not use your magic for this quest?"

"Wait, I can use magic to travel?" Travis asked, his eyes sparkling.

"You can use magic for anything, Travis; you are the Chosen One, so there are no boundaries for you. If you have a spell, you must use it. Time depends on it!" Zarf said nervously.

"We will get to that mountain in about ten minutes," Travis said, looking at the terrain in front of them. "We'll take a break then and I'll see what I can do."

With the plan in place, they carried on walking until they reached the foot of the mountain, where they sat down to rest and think about what magic Travis could use.

Removing his backpack, Travis reached into it, pulling out two bottles of water and two bananas. He passed a bottle of water and a banana to Zarf and explained what they were.

After having eaten the banana and after drinking half the bottle of water, Travis tightened the cap and put it into his backpack, saving the rest for later. "We need some sticks or logs in order for me to do my next spell," he announced, before heading off towards the trees on his left.

Zarf watched as Travis laid the sticks alongside one another on the ground, then began fastening them together with string. He pulled out his plinth, pointed it at the sticks, and started mumbling.

"Fluba – toroto – to fley!" Travis whispered, watching as the sticks began to lift off the ground.

"A flyer!" exclaimed Zarf. "You're brilliant, Travis! Now we can fly and save time searching!"

"You think I'm brilliant?" asked Travis, a small smile playing on his lips.

"No, but you're a quarter of the way there," Zarf replied, and with that the two bursts out laughing.

Once they'd both calmed down, Travis jumped onto the flyer, with Zarf following close behind. The flyer began to vibrate, and then up they slowly began to rise.

Travis was just holding his compass up to make sure they were heading in the right direction, when suddenly, a bright light started beaming out from the neck line of Travis's shirt.

"The green stone is awakening, Travis," Zarf said.

"We must be closing in on one of the stones," Travis replied, his heart skipping a beat at the thought.

Just then, the stone began to emit a sharp, high-pitched whistle. "Can you hear that, Zarf?" Travis asked.

"Hear what? All I can hear is a strange buzzing sound," Zarf replied. It was like the sound a metal detector makes when you're searching for something in the ground: the closer you get, the louder the pitch becomes, with the sound fading as you go off course.

Slowly and cautiously, Travis brought the flyer down to land, and once they'd both hopped off, Travis pulled the necklace up with the green stone attached to it. As he did so, a huge beam of green light lit up the sky.

It was magnificent, but the screeching noise was getting too much for Travis and he held the stone away from his body as far as he could. With the stone in his left hand, he began to follow the beam, which was now pointing directly to a rock underneath an average, leafy tree about 50 metres to his left.

"I bet that's where one of the six stones is trapped!" Travis said. "Let's go and see!"

Before either of them could take a step forwards, however, a bright blue beam of light shot up into the sky out of nowhere. It was followed by a loud scream, and then the stone flew through the air, landing just a few metres away from the rock. It was still shining brightly into the sky. Travis and Zarf looked at each other and frowned.

"What was that?" Travis asked, his voice shaking.

"I've heard that type of scream before, Travis; it was the same sound I heard when Trogg was banished by Murtic! We'd better be careful," Zarf said in a whisper.

They both walked over very quietly, so as not to frighten whatever was hiding behind the rock. Travis had just bent down to pick up the blue stone and put it in his pocket when a voice suddenly appeared out of nowhere.

"Please don't hurt me; I was sent here by Murtic," the voice said, followed by a thin and bony arm that appeared with a stretched-out hand, followed by the tip of two pointy ears and then two big, round eyes.

"Trogg!" shouted Travis. "It's you; we've been searching all over for you!"

"For me? You have? Why?" Trogg asked, looking incredibly confused.

"Well," replied Travis, "we're searching for the stones of Zar, and we'd like you to join us as part of our team," he added, trying to make Trogg feel wanted.

"Me, Trogg? Part of the team? Oh, yes please! Make me part of the team!" Trogg shouted happily, jumping up and down as excitement and joy beamed from his big, round eyes.

"Travis," Zarf whispered, "you have to give him something that belongs to you – if he accepts it, you will be his master and he will serve you with great honour."

Reaching into his backpack, Travis pulled out a coloured button and held it out towards Trogg.

Trogg looked at it intently. "You are giving me something special of yours; you want Trogg to be your friend forever, oh great one?" he asked Travis.

Travis nodded as he handed over the button. "That's right."

"Yes, Trogg," Travis reiterated. "I would like you to be my friend, and once this quest is over, you can be free to do as you please."

As Trogg reached out for the button in Travis's outstretched hand, Zarf whispered once again to Travis, "The only way Trogg can truly be free is when you ask for the button back. At that point, you need to break it in two and give him half back."

Trogg touched the button and it promptly disappeared. "Trogg will protect you and honour you," he said to Travis.

Travis nodded at Trogg, before looking back at Zarf. "We must go now; we still have to find the other stones." With that, he pulled out his compass, watching for the West coordinates to track down the yellow stone. Slowly, the needle began to spin, and Travis moved around until he was in line with the compass's reading. "West!" he shouted loudly. "That is our next destination; West to find the yellow stone of Zar, let's go!" He hopped quickly onto the flyer. "Come along, Trogg! Hop up; we don't have much time left."

Once on the flyer, they all braced themselves for the West journey, and after travelling for about 35 minutes, the scenery started to change – the view went from the rough, rugged, dry landscape to a lush, green, and welcoming sight.

"I'll take the flyer down here so we can have some food and drink; we need to restore our strength," Travis said to the others. He'd spotted some trees surrounding a small but crystal-clear watering hole, and had quickly decided it would be the perfect place to rest and reenergise.

After a few seconds, Travis set the flyer down next to what appeared to be a cave. "I've not seen any sign of life in this world, and it's starting to bother me a little," Travis said to Zarf.

"Oh, great one, this world is full of life!" Trogg quickly replied, with a knowing look on his face.

"When and where did you see life, Trogg?" Travis asked.

"When I first arrived, I saw little people – they looked like you, oh great one," Trogg answered.

"Little people like me? Where are they, Trogg?" Travis asked.

"Oh, great one…"

"Please stop calling me oh great one, Trogg."

"Yes master," Trogg replied.

"And please stop calling me master too," Travis said, feeling a little uncomfortable with the whole thing.

"Yes, oh great one," Trogg replied.

"No, Trogg! Don't call me great one or master!'"

"Yes sir," Trogg replied.

At this stage, Travis didn't have the strength to argue or to explain, so he just told Trogg to call him whatever he felt comfortable with. "Now, tell me more about the little people."

"I saw them the day I arrived, master; they were out and about at time of moon, and at time of play they went underground." Trogg grinned, happy that he'd finally been given the chance to complete his sentence.

"So, they come out at night and sleep during the day, and they live underground... now that *is* strange," Travis pondered out loud.

"They must have an entire village underground – or maybe their whole world is underground," Zarf suggested, shrugging his shoulders.

"I wonder why that is?" Travis asked, more to himself than anyone else.

They all sat at the entrance to the cave as Travis started to hand out some supplies; with only two bottles of water left, Travis told Trogg that they'd have to share a bottle, which Trogg agreed to, eager to please. Travis handed Trogg and Zarf an apple each and then shared the pack of biscuits out amongst them.

"Trogg drink water from stream, Trogg no need share master's water!" Trogg said to Travis, before turning to the stream.

"Wait!" Travis shouted. "You don't know if the water is poisonous or magical, Trogg."

Trogg made a little gesture, which Travis assumed to be a shrug. "Little people drink water, Trogg drink water." And with that Trogg knelt down and scooped up some water in his hands, splashing his face before scooping up a little more to drink. "Slurp, slurp! This water is cold, Trogg like cold, sweet water."

Just then, Trogg started making some horrific noises as he screeched, "I can't see, I can't see! Ah, I'm dying… I can't breeeeeathe!" And with that, he fell down on the ground in front of Travis, where he just lay like a rag doll.

Travis peered down at him. "Trogg, I told you not to drink the water. What are we going to do, Zarf? Can you help him?"

Zarf bent down, trying to see if there was anything he could do or if it was too late to save the little Aztar. As Zarf tried to look into Trogg's eyes, however, Trogg jumped up, hopping around on one foot and then the other as he laughed out loud. "Trogg got you good, Trogg see it on faces! Trogg not really dead!" he shouted with glee.

"You silly little thing, you, what were you thinking? That was not at all funny, Trogg!" Travis shouted, with Zarf nodding furiously in agreement.

"I was only joking, Trogg funny; you should have seen the face of you two," Trogg said to Travis.

Travis sighed. "You should never play tricks like that, Trogg —next time, when you really *are* hurt, we won't believe you," he explained in an annoyed tone of voice.

With the 'drama' over, they all sat back down, drinking the water and eating the apples and biscuits. They then filled up the empty bottles with the clear water from the watering hole. Travis put the bottles in his backpack, threw it over his shoulder, and then reached into his pocket for the blue stone.

"These stones look just like marbles," he mused out loud. "Just three more stones to go and we'll be celebrating! Let's go – we need to move on." Travis put the stone back into his pocket, stood up, and pulled out his compass to make sure they were still on the right track. Pausing for a moment, Travis also pulled out the green stone and inspected it. There was nothing, not even a tiny hint of flickering light – it was clear that they weren't even close. With that, they hopped onto the flyer, and once again they were off.

"We've been travelling for hours," Travis said after what felt like forever. "The clouds are starting to darken and the day is almost over. We need to find shelter and revise our plan – after all, we're almost into the fourth day of the countdown."

Since they'd been travelling, there had been no sign of the yellow stone's whereabouts. They had, however, seen a nice-looking forest along the way – about 20 minutes back – so they decided to backtrack and set up camp for the night.

Once they'd arrived, they began to scout the area, looking for a water hole or any signs of life, like footprints or tracks, or even a house in the forest. After a while of searching, they stumbled upon a stream, but this was clearly no ordinary stream: what looked like a ladder went down under the ground nearby.

It was now getting even darker as night started to set in, and to make matters worse, rain drops had just started to pitter-patter on Travis's backpack, the early signs of an oncoming downpour. It was clear that the three travellers needed to find shelter soon, and they all agreed to explore whatever lay beneath the ground near the stream.

Before they went, Travis removed his backpack and started rummaging through it until he found the two torches he'd packed. He gave one torch to Zarf and kept the other one for himself. Then, they all stood around the ladder leading underground, staring into the depths. Whatever was down there, they were soon going to find out.

Switching on his torch, Travis started to descend down the ladder, followed closely by Trogg and then Zarf, who brought up the rear. It was a long way down and very dark, but finally they reached the bottom of the ladder, where it became a little brighter. Travis switched off his torch, then asked Zarf for the other one so he could put them away in his backpack, before they all began to walk down the corridor in front of them. This corridor led to a door, and when Travis opened it, all three of them gasped in astonishment; to their amazement it looked just like they were back above the surface, with clouds, sun, and trees.

"Wow, this is weird," Travis said to Zarf as Zarf finally walked through the door and closed it behind him.

All three of them walked out from the safety of the cave into the open and the unknown, and Travis looked around them in wonder. "We'd better remember this cave and its whereabouts, otherwise we might never find our way back," he muttered to Zarf.

-Woizle-

-Salty Holding the Box of Stones-

-Treap-

CHAPTER FIVE

THE GATES OF NETHERLESS

The next morning when all three of the little group awoke, they were met by the sunniest day any of them had seen in a long while.

After going over to the stream to wash his face, Travis sat down to breakfast with the others. "Today we must prepare for our return to Netherless land; we need to plan our next move very carefully as it will have many serious consequences and repercussions," Travis told Zarf and Trogg, who both nodded in agreement.

After a hearty breakfast, Travis sat down with the stones and decided to devise a way to keep them altogether in one place, and to eliminate the bright light that would shine when the stones were activated in any such way.

Travis sat on the ground for a long period of time, pondering how he could disguise the Stones of Zar as he opened and closed his compass, an action that helped him think.

After a while, a great idea came to him: he was going to use magic to bind the stones together within the lid of the compass. This would hide the shining stones' bright light when activated, and it would also be easy to access a new route if urgent travel was needed.

Placing his compass on the ground, Travis bent the lid as far back as possible so it was in line with the bottom half of the compass. He then placed five of the six stones in their correct sequence in the lid of the compass, before pulling out his plinth. Finally, he began twirling the end of it around in tiny circles as he said the following words: "Ente rar —de mar — deos."

When Travis tapped the compass with his plinth, a bright flash of light appeared just as the lid of the compass slammed shut. After accepting a backlash of bright colourful light that was thrown back at him, Travis was sent into a daze for a couple of seconds. "Wow, that was bright!" he exclaimed as he clutched the compass, tightening his grip around it so no one could snatch it from him. He then held his hand out, and with his other hand, he slowly began to open the lid of the compass.

When this action was completed, Travis stared at the wonderful sight of his new compass and said, "This shall now be called my pathfinder." Closing the top and pulling through a thin black string, he tied it around his neck like a necklace.

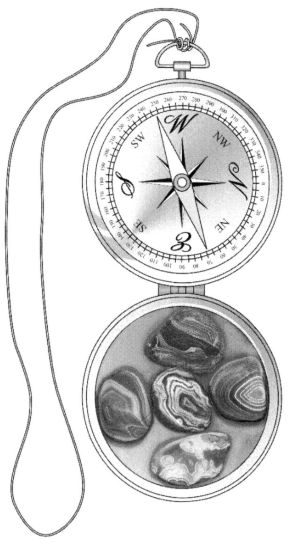

-The Pathfinder Compass-

Travis then pulled out a small pocket knife from his backpack and began sculpting his plinth. He made it as short as 15 centimetres and as thin as a pencil, then he sat for the next ten minutes carving out images onto the wood, personalising it and making it unique to him.

Travis was now starting to feel like a real wizard; everything was coming together quite nicely. He had his plinth and his pathfinder – all he needed now was the purple stone for his quest to be completed.

"Zarf, Trogg, we need to set off soon!" he shouted once he'd finished decorating his Plinth.

The other two came over, and sitting on the ground, they devised a plan of action to retrieve the purple stone and restore order to Netherless land. Once they were satisfied with what they had to do, they all climbed onto the flyer and headed towards the tree house that Travis and Zarf had stayed in before. By the time they arrived there, all three of them were feeling pretty anxious, though excited at the same time.

"The time has finally come," announced Travis. "We need to

re-enter Netherless land and reclaim the purple stone. Are you ready?"

"Oh yes, master, Trogg is ready to serve!" Trogg shouted.

"Yes, Travis, let us restore happiness to Netherless land!" Zarf replied.

Standing near to where they had entered the tree house, Travis reached down the front of his shirt and pulled out his pathfinder that hung around his neck. Holding it out in front of him, he lifted the lid and then gently touched the green stone. There was a bright flash of green light, and just as fast as you could have blinked, the trio found themselves back on top of the mountain in Netherless land. Smiling, Travis closed his pathfinder and dropped it back down the neck of his shirt.

"We're back, guys!" he exclaimed. "Everything looks quiet down there; I think it's time for a surprise visit to Murtic."

"Be quiet! I can hear some rustling in those bushes over there," Zarf whispered, before walking over and demanding whoever was there to come out, but nothing stirred.

Travis walked forwards, pulling out his plinth and saying some magic words.

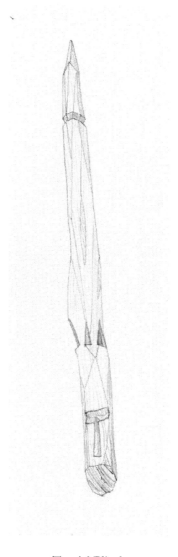

-Travis' Plinth-

"Aerah–aerah-hyy!" He pointed his plinth in the direction of the bush, and just as he'd started to lift his plinth up into the air, up floated a Glebbilin from behind the bush, shouting to be put down immediately.

"Jennith the Great Wott's daughter, is it really you?" Zarf asked, his eyes wide in surprise.

"Zarf, you didn't desert us after all!" Jennith shouted.

Realising who it was, Travis gently lowered Jennith and put away his plinth.

"Who is that, Zarf?" Jennith asked. "Who is that wizard with that magic stick?"

"This is Travis," explained Zarf. "Come over, Travis! I'd like you to meet Jennith, the Great Wott's daughter; Jennith, this is Travis the pathfinder who has found five of the six stones." Zarf introduced the two of them to each other.

"It is a pleasure to meet you, my Princess," Travis said politely.

"Princess?" Jennith repeated with a confused look upon her face but continued… "You are the pathfinder – it is such an honour to meet *you,* Travis! We've all heard about you in stories, but I never thought this day would come."

"What's happened?" Zarf asked, interrupting them. "Why are you up here, Jennith?"

Jennith lowered her head as she replied, "Murtic has taken my father prisoner, and everyone is starting to act strangely; they're stealing and arguing, while others are starting to chant 'Murtic the Great'! I just had to get away before I too fell under Murtic's spell."

"Where is Murtic now?" Travis asked, eager to get going.

"He's in the Castle of Wott with his five Aztars, Zeed, Woizle, Treap, Muftish, and Mulisty. I have no Idea where Trogg is hiding," Jennith said with a shrug.

"Trogg not hiding, Trogg over here!" Trogg shouted with a smile – he'd been standing behind Travis and Zarf the whole time they'd been talking to Jennith.

"Catch him, Zarf! It's Trogg, and I know he's up to no good!" Jennith shouted, worried.

"No, it's alright; Trogg is with us," Zarf explained. "He's serving Travis now." He then went on to tell the whole story of what had happened over the last couple of days while Jennith listened, wide-eyed.

"How do we get into the Castle of Wott?" Travis asked Jennith.

She thought for a moment. "The people are starting to protect Murtic, and they've been ordered to capture anyone they see who appears to be different or who looks like they don't belong here in Netherless land. I'll take you to my father's secret escape route. Follow me!"

With that, the trio followed Jennith all the way down the mountain to where the escape route from the Castle of Wott

…lay hidden.

"This is the Cave of Time," said Zarf. "Are you telling me that this is where the escape route leads to?"

"Yes – look what happens when you stand on that second step with one foot and then push on that third rock on the wall above the circular marking," Jennith said, gesturing for him to try.

Zarf did exactly what Jennith told him, and after a few seconds there was a rumbling sound as the centre piece of the cave slid a little to the left, exposing a flight of stairs that lead down to a dark void.

"It looks rather dark and creepy down there," Jennith said as she peered into the gap.

"No worries, I have two flash lights that will help us see the way," Travis replied as he started ruffling through his backpack for the torches. He gave one to Trogg, then made him walk behind as he went ahead with the other torch. Travis started to descend as the others followed.

They walked along the passage, soon coming to another flight of stairs, which went up in a spiral direction. At the top, however, their way was blocked by a solid wall with no entrance.

Jennith edged her way forwards, asking the others to stand back as she stepped onto a circular stepping stone and then pushed one of the rocks which made up the solid wall. The wall began to rumble slightly and then started to rotate. They all followed Jennith through as the wall slowly rotated back into place, then they walked up another flight of stairs, finally coming to a hole in the ground. Jennith told them all to jump in, and as they did just that, another wall slid back. They now found themselves in a bathroom, and they all watched in fascination as the wall with the sink and the mirror slid back into position.

"That is the best secret passageway I have ever come across!" Travis said excitedly as he put the torches away.

Jennith nodded her agreement. "Now, we have to be very quiet so as not to disturb Murtic and the others."

Heeding Jennith's warning, they all walked very quietly in the shadows towards the Great Wott's room to see if he was there. The door had two guards posted outside, which meant that he was locked inside and was carefully being watched.

Cautiously, Travis stepped forwards with his plinth in his hand as he mumbled, "Sleepither – sleeepith!" He then walked towards the guards – both of whom had now fallen asleep on the floor – and reached out for the door, but it was locked. He looked around at Jennith for help.

Rushing over, she held her hand on the door until it clicked open, then they all rushed inside, closing the door behind them.

Once they were in, Travis faced the door and mumbled, "Tremintus – tris – treeth!"

"What was that all about?" Zarf asked.

"I woke the guards up in case Murtic speaks to them – can you imagine what will happen if they're asleep when he needs them?" Travis asked.

Quietly, they followed Jennith over to a very large bed, where it looked as if someone was fast a sleep under the covers. Jennith slowly pulled away the blanket – to be sure that it was her father and not someone else lying in the bed – smiling as she saw Hop the Great Wott fast asleep. "Dad!" she shouted as she threw her arms around him.

Hop opened his eyes immediately, delighted to see her and Zarf. "Where have you been all this time, Jennith? And who is the boy?" Hop asked.

"It's a long story," Jennith replied. "Zarf will explain later. Who's in the castle with you?"

"Murtic has sent everyone away and brought in his Aztar followers," her father said sadly. "He's started using magic; he has armoured guards, which are just empty armour suits keeping watch over the castle. There are about eleven of them in total, and then there are his five closest Aztars, Muftish, Mulisty, Zeed, Woizle, and Treap."

Kneeling down beside the great Wott's bed, Travis and Zarf started to explain what had unfolded over the last few days. Hop was more than intrigued by the story of the other lands, and especially the tale of Travis the pathfinder. Hop asked Travis if he'd be able to reunite the purple stone with the other stones of Zar, and Travis assured Hop that it could be done – and that he would do it.

"Wonderful!" replied Hop. "Then let's do this!"

Smiling, Travis leaned down to whisper into Trogg's ear. "Trogg, I'm going to need your help."

-Jennith the Great Wott's Daughter-

CHAPTER SIX

GOOD VERSUS EVIL

Travis and Trogg walked over towards the door, opening it slowly and peering out into the hallway.

"Halt!"

"Who goes there?" two booming voices rang out.

"Run!" Travis shouted to Trogg, and they ran down the hallway with the two enchanted suits of armour hot on their heels.

They turned at the end of the hallway, running down another until they got to what looked like a study. They dashed inside, closing the door behind them quickly. Leaning against the polished wood, they caught their breath as they heard footsteps running past outside.

"That was close, wasn't it Trogg?" Travis whispered, waiting on an answer. When he didn't get one, he turned around and gasped. To his amazement, standing by a large fireplace and getting all warm and cosy were the five Aztars: Muftish, Mulisty, Zeed, Treap, and Woizle, all of them staring at Trogg.

Woizle stepped forwards, reaching out a hand to touch Trogg. "Is that really you, brother?" he asked. "Where did you go? We thought you'd been turned to dust, but you found your way back! How?"

"Trogg very happy," he replied. "Trogg meet Travis the great one, greater than Murtic, and now Trogg will serve new master." He held out the button that Travis had given to him.

They all came forward then, touching, poking, and prodding at Trogg – they were so happy that their brother had returned, and they were so grateful to Travis that they decided to help the great wizard with whatever was needed; Woizle – the elder of the six – made a promise to Travis that they would help in any way they could.

Travis told all of them to act as normal as possible, and to pretend that they'd not seen Trogg or Travis ever since they'd been banished days earlier – it was vital that Murtic remain in the dark about their conspiring against him. Travis also told the Aztars that they had to act as if they were against both Travis and Trogg, should they happen to be found together. Finally, he advised Woizle to alert Murtic before the guards did – to prove his loyalty to him – and to say that he'd seen them going up the mountain side.

Once the discussion was over, Travis and Trogg hid behind one of the corner bookcases while they waited for the five Aztars – Woizle, Muftish, Mulisty, Zeed, and Treap – to spread the word.

Woizle, followed by the other four Aztars, ran towards the main study – which was only used by Murtic – and banged frantically on the door.

A second later the door flew open and Murtic shouted out loud, "This had better be a matter of urgency! To come down here at this late hour and disturb me!" He looked furious.

"Master, master!" Woizle cried excitedly. "It's the magic boy! I've seen him running up the side of the mountain with Zarf;

should we go and catch them?"

Murtic frowned. "But that's impossible!" he shouted back. "They could never return... and if they did, I would know! Now, take your foolish thoughts and disappear before I make you join Trogg – or have you forgotten what I did to your brother?!" he boasted, a cruel glint in his eye.

"No, master," Woizle replied, shame in his voice. "I will leave you to your peace and quiet. Sorry, oh great one." Closing the door behind him, Woizle then walked back towards the other study, followed closely by the others. "Trogg, it's OK, you can come out now," he said.

There was no answer, and when Woizle looked behind the corner bookcase and behind the chairs, Trogg and Travis were nowhere to be seen; they had already left to prepare for their battle.

Travis and Trogg were now back with Zarf, Jennith, and the Great Wott, and they were discussing their plans to restore Netherless land to its former glory.

"Hop," said Travis, before clearing his throat. "Would it be OK if I could talk to your people? We need to prepare them to overthrow Murtic, and get ready for a great war."

Hop nodded solemnly; this was something they simply had to do.

"Right," continued Travis. "Zarf and Jennith, I need you to follow Trogg and myself back to the Cave of Time."

The others nodded, and soon they had made their way back to the Cave of Time. It was here that they really started to get to the gritty details of their plan, and before they knew it, they'd talked all night.

As the morning began to brighten up, the streets of Netherless land began to get busy. There was a loud crash as a gang of Aztars threw a garbage can through a bakery window, grabbing cakes and sweets from the display units. Others started to follow their lead – knocking over bins, arguing with one another, and taking things from shops without paying. It was chaos.

Zarf – who had been watching the crazy actions of the Aztars – decided that he couldn't take any more destruction, and that he needed to act quickly. In a flash, he disappeared and reappeared in the centre of all the commotion, then he raised his arms slowly as he began to mumble. As he did so, the clouds began to move quickly across the sky, turning grey and then black as tiny drops of rain started to fall to the ground.

"Out of the way!" cried one of the Aztar gang members. "We don't have time for magic shows!"

"Magic show?" replied Zarf. "You have no idea of the magic show you're about to get! I am Zarf, Keeper of the Stones of Zar and Watcher over the Cave of Time!" He shouted this for all to hear, the morning growing darker as the drops of rain got steadily bigger and heavier. Everyone stopped what they were doing, looking upwards to the heavy skies.

Suddenly, one of the Aztars shouted for everyone to run, but it was too late – the rain drops turned to gloop, sticking everyone to the ground, stopping them in their tracks – the gloop was so heavy and sticky that it pinned them to wherever they were standing or sitting at the time.

Looking around him, Zarf lowered his arms as he said, "This was a warning! Now, clean up and restore normality to Netherless land or you will face more spells – and, my good Aztar people, this will not be a magic show!" With that, Zarf disappeared in a flash, leaving everyone wide-eyed and open-mouthed.

Murtic – who had heard all the commotion – quickly summoned his Aztar followers, who all came and stood before him as he spoke.

"Woizle, I have heard talk that Zarf, the Keeper of the Stones, has reappeared in Netherless land. Now, you told me that you'd seen Zarf and the magic boy, so I want you to find them and bring them to me. The time has come to put things right – once and for all. Guards, I want you to watch my every move. Now leave!"

Meanwhile, back in the Cave of Time, plans were coming together very nicely.

"We need a distraction, something to draw Murtic out into the open," Travis said.

"I have a plan," Zarf replied, and with that he ran out into the town square once again.

Zarf moved his hands this way and that, pointing his bony little finger up to the sky and then down towards the ground, to the left and then to the right. In an instant, the winds started to pick up, howling over other new noises: the clatter and banging of dirt bins, and anything else not tied down as it started to get thrown all over the place. Pot plants rose into the air and smashed against walls as water from the drains lifted into the air and sprayed across Netherless land.

Now that they could move again, the Glebbilins and the Aztars were running for cover; they hid in shops, under benches, in each other's homes, and some even tried to find refuge amongst the old sacred ruins of Zar, the most forbidden place for anyone to set foot upon.

Murtic was furious that the magic boy and Zarf, Keeper of the Stones of Zar, had managed to find their way back from the banished land – they had gone against his wishes and were now upsetting his plans. They had to be stopped.

Murtic summoned his guards – as his five Aztars were out looking for Travis and Zarf – and once they'd been rounded up, they all marched off to confront their enemies. Two guards lead the way while an army of 20 followed from behind.

With a blink of an eye, Zarf returned to the Cave of Time and re-joined the others. "Now is the time to finally meet face to face with Murtic and put an end to this nonsense," said Travis, looking around at the others. They nodded in confirmation.

So, while Travis and Zarf went to meet with Murtic, the Great Wott and his daughter Jennith went to meet with some of the people who Trogg had managed to gather in the Netherless land underground storage facility. This storage facility was where they stored emergency supplies from the early harvest, should bad times ever fall upon Netherless land.

Hop addressed the crowd. "We're going to overthrow Murtic, so you need to prepare for a great war like the war many, many moons ago, which separated the Glebbilins and the Aztars! Now is the time to rebuild and become the peaceful land we once were! We shall protect our existence as Glebbilins of Netherless land against the dark and evil forces of Murtic!"

There was a roaring cheer from the crowd, and a thunderous boom of clapping hands as they all agreed.

At the same time, Travis and Zarf stood firm at the Cave of Time as they awaited Murtic's arrival.

After a while, the streets began to rumble, and the buildings began to tremble and shake as the marching Aztar guards approached with Murtic. As they drew nearer to the cave, the procession looked like a river of silver water flowing through the street.

They stopped just in front of Travis and Zarf, and as the two leading guards moved aside, Murtic emerged and stepped forwards.

"So, you found a way back from the banished land, how lucky!" cried Murtic sarcastically, "But I'm afraid it's too late – the time is drawing near, and nothing will stop me or the Aztars from turning this land to the way of the Aztar life, just as it was many, many moons ago. Guards, take them to the Castle and await my further orders!" he ordered.

"Not so fast, you spiky, grey-haired little man!" shouted Travis. "Do you think it's that easy to defeat two powerful wizards?" He smiled at Murtic. "Have you not asked yourself how we could have found our way back from being banished? Well, have you?" he cried.

"Ha ha haaaa," came Murtic's reply. "I have the purple stone of Zar, so I don't need to ask anything of anyone, you foolish little boy! I know your magic – or should I say 'trickery'. You see, you cannot have magic where you come from, so you may be able to fool everyone else, but you cannot fool me! I am the most powerful of all!" He turned to his guards again. "Take them away! And find me those five Aztars – I want them brought to the castle for their own banishment!"

Despite his showing off, Murtic was worried and pretty scared – after all, he had no idea how they'd both returned from the banished land. He knew, however, that he couldn't show any of the fear he felt – if he did, he would lose his status and his followers would start to defy him.

Travis, on the other hand, knew exactly what was going on inside Murtic's head; he knew that Murtic was confused and worried, and that was good – that's just what he needed for his next plan.

-Hop the Great Wott-

Just then, Travis and Zarf were grabbed by both arms and marched off to the castle, while six of the other guards went off in search of the five Aztars. They went willingly, not putting up a fight – yet.

The Great Wott and Jennith now were in the Netherless land underground storage facility, where they had been advised to stay out of Murtic's sight. The Glebbilins had gone to spread the word about the Great Wott's plan and how the Prophecy of the "pathfinder" was coming true.

For his part, Trogg was following the guards at a distance to see where they were taking Travis and Zarf, while at the same time, Murtic was waiting for the other guards to return with the five Aztars. He heard the marching of the guards and the mumbling of the Aztars as they entered the hallway.

"You five Aztars!" Murtic yelled. "Woizle, Muftish, Mulisty, Zeed, and Treap, you have all disappointed me for the last time! You have lied to me, you have plotted against me, and now you shall be banished to the same place where your raggedy brother Trogg is!" He sneered, pointing his purple stone at the five Aztars in front of him, and a bright purple light shone upon the five as they huddled together.

They looked scared, and just as the light hit them, Woizle shouted, "No, your greatness! Please do not banish us! We will beeeeeeeeeeee…" And with that, they were gone, Woizle unable to even finish his sentence.

Murtic nodded to himself. "Now it's just me and the guards, and whichever Aztars are willing to turn against the Glebbilins."

Trogg was hiding behind the castle gatehouse, when all of a sudden, Woizle, Muftish, Mulisty, Zeed, and Treap appeared next to him in a bright flash.

"Where did you all come from?" he asked in a squeaky voice, their sudden appearance having made him jump.

"Murtic banished us to where you were," explained Zeed, "but of course, he didn't realise you were back in Netherless land."

Realising what had happened, they all began grinning and twitching with excitement. The plan to banish the five Aztars had backfired, and now they were going to spread the word about Murtic: how he uses the Aztar people at his disposal and how he doesn't have their best interests at heart – or any interests, in fact. So off they went, and word soon got around about what had happened to the five Aztars. People were starting to become rather unsettled.

Trogg made his way to Travis and Zarf, who were now being guarded at the top of the castle.

"Trogg!" exclaimed Travis. "How did you find us? Where are the others?"

"Woizle, Muftish, Mulisty, Zeed, and Treap are spreading the word about Murtic amongst the Aztars, and the Great Wott and Jennith are keeping out of sight – as you said, master."

Travis nodded, smiling. "Zarf, I think the time has come for us to reunite the purple stone with the others, and to restore order to Netherless land."

With that, Travis removed three bed sheets from the bed and lay them down on the floor in front of him. He then took out his plinth, and pointing it at the three sheets, he began mumbling.

"Vladee – flarish – vaneesh!" The sheets immediately turned transparent. "Zarf, Trogg – pick up a sheet each and use it like an invisibility cloak. Don't worry; we'll be able to sneak past the guards."

Intrigued, the two picked up a sheet each as Travis picked up the third, and upon throwing them around themselves like a cloak, they all promptly became invisible.

"Wow!" shouted Zarf. "This is unbelievable!"

Ignoring Zarf's enthusiasm, Travis faced the door with his plinth and mumbled, "Sleepither – sleeepith! Right, let's go." Opening the door, he and the others slowly sneaked past the guards, then before they left, Travis turned and pointed towards the guards with his plinth once again, mumbling, "Tremintus – tris – treeth!" A moment later, the guards awoke from their sleep.

They made their way down the passages of the castle as fast as they could, heading towards the Cave of Time, but when they reached the entrance, they found that it was closed up – nothing would open it for entry.

"Something's wrong, Zarf," whispered Travis, frowning. "The Cave of Time won't open!"

-Aztar Warrior-

CASTLE of WOTT

Zarf thought for a moment. "I think someone may have walked in the old sacred ruins of Zar, the most forbidden place for anyone to set foot upon… The Keeper of the Stones of Zar – the Watcher over the Cave of Time – may use the footpath in times of need, but only in desperate times, otherwise the Cave of Time will close up to protect the Stones of Zar," he explained.

"How do we reopen the cave?" asked Travis desperately.

"We can't," replied Zarf, shrugging sadly. "All the stones need to be in one place – together and in the Cave of Time itself – otherwise the cave will be sealed off forever. We have to get the stones inside the cave before the second time of moon, or life for the Glebbilins as we know it will have changed forever!"

Travis rubbed his chin, trying to think. "We need to act fast; time is running out! Each time we're met with obstacles, they slow us down. Look, I'll head towards Murtic to try and retrieve the purple stone, while you go and find the Great Wott. Trogg, you can come along with me – we're going to give Murtic a little surprise."

"Hee hee, master! This will make Trogg happy, very happy!" came the reply.

Without waiting another second, they wrapped the sheets around them again and off they headed. Travis and Trogg soon reached the main part of the castle where Murtic was thinking up a plan, and there were now about 50 Aztar guards standing there – now looking more like warriors than ever before.

Travis quietly walked towards the door where the guards were standing and slowly turned the door handle, hoping they wouldn't hear him. Opening the door, Travis and Trogg sneaked into the room, still covered in their invisibility sheets.

"Who's there?" shouted Murtic instantly. "I know someone's here, show yourself!"

Right on cue, Travis dropped the invisibility sheet, standing in front of Murtic with a smile on his face. "Hello Murtic, surprised to see me? I have someone else here who'd like to say hello."

Just then, Trogg dropped his own invisibility sheet that he'd been wrapped in. "Hello Murtic, old dusty one! Hee hee hee!" Trogg laughed.

"HOW DARE YOU!" roared Murtic. "How dare you call me names when you address me! You will address me as the great one!" He paused for a moment, a wicked grin creeping over his mouth. "Let's see… this time I won't banish you; I'll disintegrate you so you no longer exist, foolish one! Your family have been banished and will never return, and now you will be forgotten forever!"

"Well well well, Murtic," said Travis, shaking his head. "I'm afraid your number's up – you need to hand over the purple stone. It's of no use to you now anyway. I am Travis the pathfinder, chosen to restore Netherless land to its former glory. Which is exactly what I'm doing. It's over, Murtic."

"Over! I'll say when it's over, and it hasn't even begun!" he screeched, as he pulled the purple stone from his pocket and pointed it at Travis, who lit up like a giant purple star. Then, Murtic pointed his bony little finger at Trogg and said, "I'll deal with you next!"

Trogg jumped up, hiding behind one of the chairs as he mumbled, "You'll be sorry Murtic, Oh great foolish one."

Just then, Travis reached up and pulled out his compass that had been tied around his neck. He slowly began to lift the top of it, and when it flung open, a rainbow of lights exploded from within, showering everything around it. The purple light started to change colour as it slowly mixed in with the other five stones.

The new silvery colour started to travel towards Murtic, and after an immense explosion of bright light, he started to turn translucent. As he realised what was happening, he dropped the purple stone as he started to fade. "What's happening to me?! Wizard boy, stop this now! I can't feel my face! Stop this nowwwwwwwwwww!" And with that, Murtic disappeared.

The stone dropped to the floor with a clatter, landing right in front of Travis. He peered down at it, frowning. "This seems too easy... something's not right here. Where did Murtic go, exactly?"

Shrugging, Travis grabbed the stone, putting it on top of the other stones inside the compass. He watched, fascinated, as it turned to a jelly-like substance, moulding with the rest of the stones. They were now all bound together in one place, which was great, but two questions still lingered in Travis's mind: where was Murtic? And what was he planning?

CHAPTER SIX

TE CAVE OF TIME

There was a commotion it the town surrounding the Cave of Time; all of Murtic's guards had gathered at the cave, and now some of the bad Aztars had also joined to support Murtic's move to overthrow the Great Wott of Netherless land.

Zarf reached the Cave of Time just as the others did: The Great Wott, Jennith, Woizle, Muftish, Mulisty, Zeed, Treap, and all of the Glebbilins. The rest of the Aztar people had also started to trickle out from their hiding places and had begun to fill the streets.

Travis and Trogg were the last to reach the cave.

"Zarf, what's happening?" Travis asked.

Zarf shook his head angrily. "We played right into Murtic's hands! He knew you had the time stones all along, and when you produced the five of them, the purple stone teleported him into the heart of the Cave of Time – just as he wanted. With the stones on the outside and Murtic in the very heart of the Cave of Time, he might be able to teleport anywhere at any time to snatch the stones and return to the heart of the cave. He will become the most powerful time keeper that Neverless land has ever known! This must never happen," Zarf added solemnly.

Just then, there was a mighty bang from within the cave, and all of the guards started rounding up the whole of Netherless land. Several of the Aztar people joined up with Murtic's guards, directing everyone back to Netherless land's underground storage facility.

After everyone had been led to the facility the doors were closed behind them and locked, an action that caused instant panic, with everyone squabbling and shouting at each other in fear.

"STOP!" yelled the Great Wott of Netherless land, getting everyone's attention. "We must not fight amongst ourselves – that is exactly what Murtic wants."

"The Great Wott is right," interrupted Jennith. "We need to stand together as one. After all, we are Netherless land, the land for all to enjoy, a place where we can live together side by side!" She looked around at the faces in front of her, hoping she was getting through to them.

They all glanced at each other – Aztars and Glebbilins alike –and slowly, they started to smile.

"We'll work together!" shouted one of them.

"We'll restore normality to this great land!" yelled another.

"With the Chosen One guiding us, we can do it!"

"Chosen One… Chosen One… Chosen One!" The chanting got louder and louder as more people joined in, and Travis took a step backwards, surprised.

"Travis, they're talking about you!" shouted Zarf in glee. "The pathfinder, the Chosen One, the one that's been prophesised!"

Travis, however, wasn't quite as enthusiastic. "I need time, I need to get my head around this – I need to work out a plan," he mumbled, shaking his head.

Zarf nodded before turning to the others. "Please, let's give the Chosen One some space so he can think!"

And with that, they all dispersed, running off to do little jobs, such as collecting food and water. For their part, the Great Wott and Jennith made sure that no one could get in or out of the underground storage facility.

Everyone ran about madly while Woizle, Muftish, Mulisty, Zeed, Treap, Trogg, Zarf, and Travis were devising a plan. They simply had to defeat the maniacal sorcerer Murtic and all of his deranged plans – and as soon as possible.

Travis now had all six stones of Zar, as well as all the wizard powers and knowledge bestowed upon him by Orgus. All Travis had to do now was understand them to their full potential.

Slowly and carefully, Travis started to experiment with the stones, and soon he realised that he could telepathically move things. The more he tried, the better he got, but he still needed a plan – just how was he going to confront the maniacal sorcerer, Murtic?

"We need to draw the guards' attention away from the Cave of Time," Travis said to Zarf, after thinking through all of their options. "I need to get close to the cave so I can try and communicate with Murtic."

Zarf nodded. "I know how to draw the guards' attention away from the cave. Woizle, Muftish, Mulisty, Zeed, Treap, and Trogg – you must go and attract the guards' attention so Travis can get near the cave."

Travis sighed. "But how? We're locked in here! There's no way out… it's impossible!" He shrugged.

"No, it's not, Travis," said Zarf in what he hoped was an encouraging tone of voice. "You must try teleporting the six Aztars outside of this underground storage facility. You have that ability now; you just need to find it! But be warned – this is one of the most dangerous of all your abilities. Should you not harness the energy correctly, you will disappear for all eternity and never be heard from again." He said this casually, as if it were no big deal – in reality, he didn't want to scare Travis.

Travis stared at Zarf for a moment, trying to get his head

around what he'd just said. "If I can teleport others, does that mean I can teleport myself? Or objects?" he asked finally.

"I'm not sure, Travis – you may only be able to teleport objects along with yourself and not them on their own. While I know that this is very dangerous, I don't know the exact workings of it." He shrugged. "I've heard about it but I've never actually encountered it before. This is all up to you now, Travis."

Travis spent the next 20 minutes trying to teleport the Aztars to the outside. He tried one by one, and he tried with all six together, but it just wasn't happening. It was incredibly frustrating.

Travis walked up to the Aztars – who were now all huddled together – and put his arms around them to join in the circle. He'd just apologised for not being able to teleport them, when all of a sudden, every single one of them vanished into thin air.

Zarf let out a loud shriek. "He did it! The pathfinder has finally done it! They're out!"

As Zarf was saying those words, Murtic was in the heart of the Cave of Time, telepathically giving orders to his guards.

"Where is that boy?" he asked angrily, his eyes closed as he tried to communicate with the outside. "I need those stones! I need to get out of here!"

Travis and the six Aztars appeared on the outside of the storage facility, and once they'd all got their bearings, Travis instructed, "This is what we're going to do. Woizle, Muftish, and Mulisty, you need to distract the guards and lead them away, back up to the castle. Zeed, Treap, and Trogg, you need to get the rest of the Aztars to follow you back to the storage facility. Open the doors, and once you're inside, close the doors behind the Aztars. The Great Wott has a plan for them. Trogg, you must then head on back to meet up with me at the old sacred ruins of Zar."

With all of them in agreement about what they had to do, they split up and went their own ways, while Travis hid behind a bush and waited. The guards turned and chased Woizle, Muftish, and Mulisty, while the Aztars chased after Zeed, Treap, and Trogg, just as planned. Four guards stood firm, but Travis had an idea of how he could get past them. Pulling out his plinth, he pointed it at the guards as he mumbled, "Sleepither – sleeepith!" before slowing walking towards the old sacred ruins of Zar.

When Travis reached the pathway to the sacred ground, he

took a deep breath before stepping cautiously onto the path, and he had just started walking towards the statue of Zar when he began to feel a strange, tingly sensation rising up through his body. He carried on, but when he reached the statue, he sat down – he was feeling too tingly to continue. As he rested, Travis heard a banging sound coming from the base of the statue, and when he put his ear closer to the stone, he promptly got sucked in – right into the statue itself.

Murtic was standing in front of him. "It's you!" Travis cried. "Why are you still playing these games? It's over! The stones are going to be placed back in the Cave of Time where Zarf will continue to watch over them."

"I will never let that happen," replied Murtic, glaring at Travis. "I've worked far too hard for far too long to get this close and lose!"

With that, Murtic raised his arms, and the compass from around Travis's neck ripped from the string it was tied to, heading straight for Murtic's raised hand. Just as he tried to grab hold of it, however, Travis used his plinth to make the object speed up, causing Murtic to grab at fresh air as it wooshed past him. The compass then hovered above both of them for a second or so, before – in a blinding flash – it imploded on itself and was gone.

"NO!" shouted Murtic, enraged. "What have you done? You foolish boy wizard!"

"What have I done?" repeated Travis, shocked. "What have you done? It's gone! Gone forever because of your greed and evil ways! Well, at least Neverless land is back to normal," he added, shrugging.

"I have not finished with you, boy wizard; I will rule Neverless land!" Murtic yelled back, and then – with a click of his fingers – he too was gone.

Travis started to walk from the statue of Zar down through the dark passages and across to the Cave of Time, and as he approached, he realised he could hear a high-pitched whistling sound. It was a sound he'd heard before, but where? He couldn't quite place it, but after a second or so, it all came flooding back.

"I remember that sound!" Travis said to himself as he walked into the cave. "The day I found the green stone… it called out to me. That means that the stones must be calling me again! I need to find them!"

Travis started searching everywhere, desperately trying to find out where the sound was coming from. Then, he saw it: a faint green light shining through a crevasse in the rock face. Getting hopeful now, he started climbing towards the green light, and once he was near, he held his hand over the crack as he closed his eyes. A second later, Travis was flung backwards, landing on the ground with a loud thump. He was knocked out instantly.

After a long while, Travis started to come around. He was a little shaky, but he stood up, dusted himself off, and immediately looked around for the green light. Still feeling quite dazed, he sat back down, accidentally landing on something, some kind of hard object. When he looked down and saw what it was, he couldn't quite believe it: it was his compass. Reaching down, he picked up the compass and lifted the lid.

There they were: all six coloured stones.

Elated, Travis put it in his pocket, but when he tried to walk out of the cave, he couldn't – he was stuck in the Cave of Time.

CHAPTER EIGHT

THE IMPOSSIBLE BATTLE

Trogg made his way back to the Cave of Time, but it was still closed up. Leaning into the rock, he listened carefully, and he could just about hear Travis calling out. Unfortunately, there was nothing he could do, so he just sat by the cave entrance and waited for it to open.

Zarf, the Great Wott, Jennith, Zeed, and Treap were all getting ready for the great war against the followers of Murtic; with about 80 Glebbilins and 30 Aztars, they began to arm themselves with weapons. The 20 Aztar followers that had been brought back by Zeed, Treap, and Trogg earlier were now locked in one of the harvest rooms, out of sight. The 46 guards of Murtic were back at the castle, searching for Woizle, Muftish, and Mulisty.

Murtic had been expelled from the Cave of Time and was now back at the castle where he'd summoned the guards to brief them on what had happened. Murtic's sorcery wasn't as powerful without the stones, but he was going to take on Zarf and Travis regardless; with his guards and his magic, he just might stand a chance.

Once they were ready, Murtic and his guards began their march down towards the storage facility, where the great Wott and Zarf were getting ready for the attack. It was now or never.

The guards broke down the doors and Murtic made his dramatic entrance, destroying all the harvests that were being kept in the storage rooms before ordering his guards to take the Great Wott and Jennith away to the castle. He hadn't counted on Zarf, however, who stood up and began using his own magic spells against Murtic; Zarf lifted him up and threw him to one side, but just before he could cast another spell, the guards seized him. Murtic got up, and after floating over to Zarf, he hit him so hard with a sleep spell that Zarf just fell to the floor.

"Take him away to the castle! And don't leave him alone at any time," he ordered.

Meanwhile, Zeed and Treap had escaped and were on their way to the Cave of Time to find Trogg. Along the way they bumped into Woizle, Muftish, and Mulisty – now they were all together once again.

As they walked, Trogg heard a noise behind him, and when he turned to look, he was surprised to see all of his brothers and sisters. He was so happy that he shrieked with joy.

"Where is the wizard?" asked Muftish.

"He's stuck inside the Cave of Time and cannot get out," explained Trogg.

Just then, Travis communicated with Trogg telepathically, telling him that they might be the key to getting him out. Travis continued explaining to Trogg what he needed to do: he had to tell each one of them to stand on each side of the cave, but two in front and two at the back. Trogg told them and they spread out just as Travis had asked. As they focused on the Cave of Time, their eyes shone up like the stones of time and the door magically opened – Travis was able to walk free.

"Trogg, it worked!" shouted Travis. "You, your brothers, and your sisters are all connected to the Cave of Time." He laughed. "All this time, the key to everything had been right here in Netherless land – you six Aztars!"

Now Travis was free, he sat down with the six Aztars and started to devise a new plan, and once everything was settled, Travis headed back towards the storage facility to end Murtic's evil doings.

As Travis approached Murtic and his guards – who were eagerly waiting in anticipation – he turned to Woizle, Muftish, Mulisty, Zeed, Treap, and Trogg. Pulling out his plinth, he pointed it at the six and mumbled a few words. With that, the six Aztars grew to be about eight-foot-tall, and each of them were covered in armour, the colour of which resembled the six stones.

After getting used to their big transformation, they all continued with their journey towards the storage facility. Now that they were so tall, Murtic saw them in the distance and immediately began his sorcery: he called on demons from the sky, and on strange creatures from beneath the earth, creating an army of evil right before their very own eyes.

Travis and his six Aztars, however, were also ready, and they commenced in the battle against good and evil.

Every spell cast by Murtic was countered by Travis, and every spell cast by Travis made him more and more powerful.

Woizle, Muftish, Mulisty, Zeed, Treap, and Trogg were having a battle of their own against the other half of Murtic's evil clan. Woizle, Muftish, and Treap were attacked from behind by eight evil Aztars.

As each of the six brave Aztar warriors started to fall one by one, and were banished to an unknown and far-off destination, you could see the individual stones in Travis's compass shine even brighter than ever before.

After the first three of the brave Aztar warriors were banished and cut off from Netherless land and their friends, Murtic's evil clan soon quickly turned to Zeed and Mulisty who were the next in line.

Nothing was going to stop Travis!

The green light shone so brightly in Travis's stone, and whistled at such a high, intense pitch, that all the guards burst into a cloud of smoke and were no more. The red, orange, yellow, blue, and green stones shone so brightly in Travis's compass that they lit up the air around them. like a firework display on the 5th of November.

The Great Wott, Jennith, and Zarf were now free of the guards and the spells that had been holding them back. Zarf had now made his way back to the storage facility only to find that his new friends Woizle, Muftish, Mulisty, Zeed, and Treap were nowhere to be seen. Zarf realised that they had fallen into Murtic's plan, and that they had now moved on. He lowered his head in despair and shook it from side to side.

Trogg shouted to Zarf, but even though Zarf turned to cast a spell on the attackers, it was too late; Trogg fell to the ground, Travis's purple stone shining so brightly that everyone around it fell to their knees, covering their eyes from the intense glow.

"Nooooo!" Travis screamed, but it was too late – Trogg's light had been the last of the six Aztar Warriors to be extinguished.

Without thinking, Travis made a wild leap, his feet flying out from under him as he grabbed at Murtic's cloak, missing it by mere centimetres.

Travis heard Zarf screaming above him, and only then did he realise he was falling. His only hope now was to have one more swipe at the hem of the evil sorcerer's cloak, so with a last frantic cry, Travis spun around in mid-fall, swinging his hand out at one last attempt to grab hold of the material.

All Travis heard was a ripping sound as he pulled Murtic from the giant rock on which he was standing; he could see the ground rising up to meet him, but it was too late – he just wasn't fast enough to use his magic powers.

Travis was so caught up in the moment of Trogg's light going out that for an instant – just one tiny instant – he forgot he was a pathfinder. He forgot that he had powerful magic that could defeat the maniacal sorcerer Murtic, who had set his sights on becoming the ruler of Netherless land by turning all good to evil. He'd forgotten it all.

Travis's chest ached as a burning sensation swirled throughout his entire body, like fire sweeping through a dry wooded forest on a hot windy summer's day. Suddenly, his chest felt tight as he struggled to breathe – he could feel his air being shut off with every attempt he made to regain some oxygen, his chest throbbing with every half-breath.

Frantically screaming, Zarf jumped down and knelt beside Travis. Rubbing his palms together, Zarf held his bright, glowing, fiery hands above Travis's chest, hoping he could heal him, hoping he could help him with his breathing.

For a couple of seconds nothing happened, but then Travis felt a wave of energy sweep over him as he choked and gasped in a last, panicked attempt to breathe in some air.

Travis squinted strangely at Zarf. "Hurry!" he cried. "We need to stop Murtic!" With that, Travis pulled himself up and reached down for his plinth. Gripping it tightly, he pointed it in the direction of Murtic as he raised his arms and cried out, "I, Travis Morton, the pathfinder and Keeper of the Stones of Zar, revoke all your magical powers and return you to a humble Aztar!" He paused, taking a deep breath before shouting, "Revergi – kata – omni – linni – zweede - zar!" As soon as he said the words, Travis's plinth lit up like a bright star in the darkest of dark nights.

"Break the plinth, Travis!" cried Zarf. "Destroy it! Break it in two! This will destroy Murtic's magic forever!"

Travis took the plinth in two hands, and just as Zarf had instructed him, he broke it over his left knee. Once it had been destroyed, he reached into his pocket, pulling out his compass and opening it. "I demand that Murtic never finds his way back to magic ever again!" he shouted, watching as the compass lit up – the purple stone shining twice as bright as the other five.

At that moment Murtic stood up and pointed at Travis, but before he could say anything, the purple stone shone a beam of light directly at Murtic, turning him to stone.

The Great Wott, Jennith the Great Wott's daughter, Zarf, and the people of Netherless land were so thankful to the pathfinder, Travis Morton, that they threw a huge party in his honour.

The Cave of Time was sealed for good, and only one person held the key – a young pathfinder by the name of Travis Morton, the Keeper of the Stones of Zar.

Muftish, Mulisty, Zeed, Treap, Woizle, and Trogg would always be remembered as true heroes, and they now have special-coloured stones inserted into the "Big Tree" in their honour – which stands in the sacred garden alongside the great statue of Zar, all of them keeping watch over the Cave of Time until their return.

The few days Travis spent travelling to help his new found friends seemed like a lifetime of an adventure. Of course, now it was time for Travis to head back to the curly whirly slide that would take him back up to his new bedroom in his new house. It was now time for Travis to explore his own world and his new village before embarking on his next quest

– a quest that is just around the corner.

An adventure of mystery, magic and mystical beasts, an adventure which will lure Travis and hopefully lead him to find his six friends and return with them to Netherless land.

To this day, Murtic's stone image still stands just outside the storage facilities, pointing to the Cave of Time as a reminder that the Stones of Zar would always be watching, and that they were only a stone's throw away.

From that day on, Travis Morton was the first and only pathfinder to ever wear the Sacred Stones of Zar from the Cave of Time.

With this compass, Travis could go anywhere in time or teleport to any place anywhere, but the most impressive ability Travis gained that day was the ability to perform powerful magic spells. Travis was now a time traveller, a true pathfinder. Above all, however, he is the keeper of the Stones of Zar.

"Sometimes, to be a hero one has to face what seems the impossible battle, and sometimes one has to go to the ends of the earth to battle what seems to be the impossible!"

Don't miss Travis' next adventure;

Coming soon:

Look out for the next adventure...

TRAVIS MORTON

and the Curse of the Six Golden Rings

An adventure of mystery, magic and mystical beasts, an adventure which will lure Travis and hopefully lead him to find his six friends and return with them to Netherless land.

THE END

ABOUT THE AUTHOR

Warrick Fivaz was Born in South Africa. He left school to join the army in 1989 where he then spent the next two years as an Ops Medic. After getting married in 1997 Warrick emigrated with his wife to England in 2001. Where he now spends his free time writing short stories.

Travis Morton and The Stones of Zar is his first fiction/fantasy book to be published

Travis Morton and The Stones of Zar
are the first in a series of fantasy novels written by British
author W. A. Fivaz

The novels will chronicle the lives of a young boy wizard,
Travis Morton and his new found friends Zarf, Trogg and
others, all of whom are Glebbilins from Netherless land, a
place where Wizardry and Time travel go hand in hand…

Printed in Great Britain
by Amazon